DR. EMMA'S
IMPROBABLE
HAPPENINGS

By

Linda B. Myers

Enjoy the journey

Linda B Myers

ABOUT THIS BOOK

Dr. Emma's Improbable Happenings is a work of historical fiction, set among actual locations and events of the early 1900s. Characters, names, and happenings are from the author's imagination. Any resemblance to actual persons - living or dead - is entirely coincidental.

No part of this book may be used without written permission, except in the case of brief quotations in critical articles and reviews. Email inquiries to myerslindab@gmail.com.

Published by Mycomm One
©2020 Linda B. Myers

Cover design by www.introstudio.me
Interior design by Heidi Hansen
Cover painting of the SS Clallam by unknown artist; object ID PS261; Courtesy Puget Sound Maritime Historical Society and Museum of History & Industry, Seattle

ISBN: 978-1-7352477-0-0

For updates and chatter:
www.LindaBMyers.com
Facebook.com/lindabmyers.author
myerslindab@gmail.com

DEDICATION

To my critique group,
Heidi Hansen
Melee McGuire
Jill Sikes

CONTENTS

PART ONE

SS *Clallam* Castaway

Port view of SS *Clallam*, PSM 1980.2.192.2,
Puget Sound Maritime Historical Society

CHAPTER ONE

The Prescott Boarding House, Seattle
July, 1902

Emma Prescott hustled in with two sizzling beef steaks and slid them in front of the outlaws. Grease dripped onto the linen tablecloth where the slabs of meat overhung their platters. Emma backed away and leaned against the dining room wall. She pressed her hands behind herself to keep them from trembling where the men could see. No reason they should know how scared she was. Or how angry.

Ma emerged from the kitchen next. She slapped down a tray of griddle cakes and potatoes, crossed her large chapped arms over her bosom, and growled, "Never had a break-in at breakfast before."

Both men were filthy, covered in dust from hard travel. One laughed at Ma's comment. "I like a lady with wit, ma'am. I surely do. A man misses that in prison. Female chatter. Right, Cutter?"

The other man grunted then stuffed his mouth with beef. The knife he used was not part of Ma's cutlery, Emma was sure as eggs is eggs about that. It was a hunting knife, a weapon to kill an elk, a bear, or a man.

The talkative one gave Emma and her mother orders. "Sit here next to me, ma'am, and you, young lady, beside gram-maw down there." Gran was at the far end of the table, staring old lady daggers toward the bandits although her eyes were so weak, Emma doubted she could actually see the men.

Emma was not used to hearing men give Ma orders. For all her eighteen years, Emma had mostly heard it the other way around. Ma took no codswallop from her boarders.

The two outlaws, reeking of sweat and horse, occupied a curved end of the oblong dining room table. Three boarders were shoved to one side to make room for the fugitives and the rifles they leaned against the table. Misters Hunt, Hardinger, and Combes were now cheek-by-jowl on the other side of Gran.

Mr. Combes silently picked up a napkin and pressed it against the ear wound he'd received from the tip of the silent one's knife. Blood dripped steadily into his collar.

Goodness. Grease and blood to wash away. What bother! Emma realized her mind must be reeling if it was dithering about laundry at a time like this. She was afraid of these intruders but fascinated as well. Imagine taking anything you want from anyone you want and whacking the folks who get in your way. She could think of a few candidates for a good whacking herself.

Emma dared to speak. "Please, sir. May I address Mr. Combes' wound?"

"Him? Naw. We'll tie 'em up in the cellar when the eatin's done. You tend to him then."

The high starched collar of Ma's pinstriped blouse pushed her double chin upward as she sat arrow-straight on the hard backed chair. "So we'll have the pleasure of your company later in the day, as well?"

This time the talker guffawed, spitting bits of flapjack and gristle onto his plate. "What's your name anyway, ma'am?"

"I am the widow Prescott. Mrs. Minerva Prescott." Ma stiffened her outraged posture all the more. Emma thought she could be less belligerent, but that was not her mother's way.

"Pleased to meet you, Minnie. This hombre here is Lewis. Last name, I guess. Maybe first. Mostly called Cutter for what he can do with a knife."

Cutter quartered two griddle cakes and stuffed the pieces into his mouth without looking up from his plate.

"Not a polite bone in his body, I'm afraid. But me? Hate lawmen. Don't care about other men either, as soon shoot 'em as smile at 'em. But I like the company of ladies. You, Minnie, put me in mind of my mother."

"Proof there is a God, sir, that I am not."

He snorted, but Emma saw the flint in his eyes. "Now ma'am. You know who you're chattin' with?"

"Of course I know who you are, young man. I am capable of reading. That is all it takes to know who you are. You are the outlaw Harry Tracy and may well murder us all."

"Didn't I just say you remind me of Ma? Do you think I'd murder my own mama? Do what I ask, and none of you ladies will be harmed in any way."

He turned to the three boarders. "Can't say the same for these gents." With that, he took out a pistol and shot Mr. Hunt between the eyebrows. Then he finished his breakfast in silence.

* * *

Ma led the way to the cellar as Mr. Hardinger helped Cutter Lewis, or Lewis Cutter, drag Mr. Hunt's body down the backstairs. Watched by Harry Tracy, Emma accompanied Mr. Combes to the kitchen and cleaned his wound with carbolic acid to sterilize the ear where a slice of lobe was missing. Then she applied an ointment she had made of yarrow mixed with goldenrod and bandaged the wound with a clean rag around his head.

"Get on with your chores now," Tracy said to her. "I'll tie this man in the cellar with the other one. You know what will happen to your ma and gram-maw if you disappear, don't you?"

"Yes, sir," she said. She didn't doubt him in the least.

Tracy stared at her. "What's your name?"

"Emma."

"When's your husband due home, Emma?"

"I am not married, sir."

"Not married?" Tracy took a longer look. "That's a damn shame," he said then turned to leave the kitchen. "Come to the parlor when you're done."

Emma began the breakfast clean-up, clearing the dining table and boiling water for the dishes. As she scoured pots, tears formed in her eyes from the lye in the soap. Or maybe from the fear and anger she held inside.

She knew nothing of the one called Cutter, although he seemed to be at the other's beck and call. But Harry Tracy. His legend was huge although, as a man, he was something of a disappointment. Nothing like the untamed marauder pictured on the covers of the dime novels. The real Tracy was no more than five foot ten, skinny as a starving cur.

This was the man who'd escaped Oregon Penitentiary in Salem and headed north on a killing spree. Just yesterday, the *Seattle Daily Times* reported that compared to Tracy, Jesse James was a Sunday school teacher. A robber and a murderer of two dozen souls, primarily lawmen and prison guards. He was among the last of the Old West outlaws, a surviving member of the Wild Bunch, a genuine Hole in the Wall gang desperado. Newspapers called him totally without remorse except for one oddity: women detained by him universally called him polite.

Maybe that's why her mother didn't seem afraid of him. Maybe she believed Gran, Emma, and she would live through this. Emma hoped she was right. She would do nothing hasty to risk their safety; she would not sneak out the back and run to the authorities.

When the kitchen was in order, Emma rolled down the sleeves of her white cotton blouse, removed her apron, and brushed crumbs from her ankle length skirt. The wide cummerbund highlighted her narrow waist, but Emma knew she was no looker. When she was still in grade school, the other kids had taught her that. Nonetheless, neatness was always a virtue so she patted her hair, then rubbed a smudge from her blue steel spectacles. Four Eyes, the other children had called her among other names less kind.

The best word for her, Emma had always thought, was colorless. Her hair was mouse brown, her eyes such a pale shade of hazel that they appeared to have faded. Her brows and lashes were so light that they might as well be transparent. In fact, the only real color to her face was the blue of her steel rims plus a sprinkling of freckles. And the occasional blush. Not that she minded. Good looks often led to bad troubles, and life was hard enough for a woman on the edge of civilization. As up-to-date as Seattle was in 1902, it was still not much more than a rambunctious frontier town.

Emma heard voices in the boarding house parlor, and realized her mother must be there with Tracy and Cutter. She quietly entered the formal room to see Cutter asleep on the sofa below the front windows, sun streaking through the shutters so he appeared to be striped. His muddy boots rubbed filth into the red damask of the sofa's curved arm.

Ma and Gran were listening to Harry Tracy whose voice was raised over the commotion of Cutter's snoring, aggrandizing his escape from the Oregon Penitentiary four weeks earlier. When Tracy saw Emma, he smiled, stood politely, and told her to have a seat. "Letting Cutter get some shut eye. Then it's my turn."

"We have an empty room, Mr. Tracy. Should I prepare a bed for you?"

"Real sweet offer, Miss Emma. But don't think I'll be lettin' you three ladies all on your own."

"Are you alarmed by three helpless women, young man?" Ma seemed hell bent on making him mad. It was not the first time Emma wished her mother would bite her tongue.

Tracy merely snorted. "You are as helpless as a rabid badger, Ma'am, if you'll pardon my saying so. Now what was I pontificatin' about?" He sat back down and crossed an ankle over a knee.

Gran interrupted in that moment with a fit of coughing and gasping even louder than Cutter's snoring. Ma lifted herself from an occasional chair and went to the old woman's defense. "My mother is consumptive. She must have a session with the Spirometer to clear her lungs. We will adjourn to her room."

"Did I say you could leave?" Tracy frowned.

"Did I ask?" Ma responded, nearly lifting Gran and escorting her from the room.

Emma thought a bit of peacemaking was in order. "Gran is quite ill, you see, Mr. Tracy," she said in the pause that followed the exit. "Her lungs. Too much excitement fills them with liquid. She begins to drown."

"Sumbitch. You mean Cutter and me caused that?"

"Well, you are rather stimulating, Mr. Tracy."

"Is she gonna die?"

Emma thought for a moment, cocking her head. "I have medicinal tonics that will help her as long as she wishes. She may not always be comfortable, but she will likely outlive you, Mr. Tracy."

Maybe he tried to hide it, but she saw the fear in the way his eyes opened a bit larger. "I take it all you Prescott women have a way with words. You see my death happening soon, do you? And please, Miss Emma. Call me Harry. Since we don't have long to get to know each other."

Was it meant as a threat or was he merely informing her that they would leave soon? Beneath her long skirt, Emma crossed her ankles and pulled her feet back under her rosewood parlor chair. "Yes, I fear your demise is imminent, Mr...Harry. They will hunt you down and kill you dead."

For a moment neither spoke. Then Emma asked a question that had pricked her curiosity since the day she'd read about it. "In the newspaper, they said you cheated in a duel with your last outlaw partner. Is that the case?"

"Well, yes. But we both did. I turned too soon as we counted out the paces, that is true, only to find he'd already turned and was aiming at me. I was the better shot."

"A posse is sure to end your life in a very few days. I find that sad, Harry. Possibly it is time for you to consider good works and putting your affairs in order." She was surprised to find herself rather sympathetic toward this outlaw's limited prospects, all the while knowing he was as warm as a snake.

"I fear, Miss Emma, you are right. I intend to end it myself before they do it for me. I'll never go back to prison. Don't see another way out."

"No. Nor do I."

"Tell me. You as pig-headed as that mother of yours?"

She smiled. She had no idea what radiance a smile brought to her pale countenance. "I suppose I am, although I don't squeal aloud quite so often. You should have met Gran when she was young. I believe the term is firecracker."

"As we agree the Angel of Death is flying my way soon, and as I have developed a fondness for the womenfolk of the Prescott Boarding House, I wonder, Miss Emma, if you would do me a favor."

"Of course, Harry. I appear to have little choice."

He lowered his voice which only increased the perceived volume of the riotous snoring. "I have in my possession an item that Cutter will try to kill me for. He is awaiting the opportunity. I choose to give it to you instead."

Emma said nothing. There was nothing for her to say since "No" was not an option.

Tracy reached into his jacket pocket and pulled out a grimy little buckskin bag. He opened it, then emptied the sack onto the marble-top table next to him. A tumble of gold nuggets spread out, gleaming richly in the lamplight as they piled atop each other.

"These are Klondike nuggets, Miss Emma. Pretty as a picture."

"Indeed, they are, Harry." She had never seen anything like it. The only gold rushers she'd ever met had nothing to show for their efforts. "Are you a Klondiker then?"

"No, not I. But I killed such a foozler for these flakes and chunks. Far better I had them. And far better you have them, now. Instead of a dying man like me or a chump like Cutter. I suggest you hide them away awhile. A month or two at the very least, 'til their path has grown cold afore you sell them."

Cutter snorted, rolled onto his side, then farted. His snoring continued.

"I'd kill him now but won't mess your parlor any more than we already have. Besides, I may still need him in the days ahead."

Emma stared at the gold but made no move toward it. Was it cool to the touch? Silky or satin smooth? Or would that sought-after gleam merely burn her as it had so many others?

"Pick it all up and hide it now, afore I change my mind or Cutter sees it." The order was stern.

She shepherded the golden bits back into the bag. Then she crossed the room to a roll-top desk, and placed the bag in a folder which she stuck into a pigeon-hole. Next, she pulled out a small envelope and turned back to Harry. "I am a natural healer, Harry. This is bark of the white willow. It can help with pain should you be wounded before you have time to take your own life. It will be more valuable to you at that time than all the nuggets in the world."

* * *

When the women awoke the next morning, the outlaws were gone. Tracy told the truth; none of them had been touched.

Emma's first job was to scamper down to the cellar to release Mr. Hardinger. As she unbound the wretched fellow, Ma went for the authorities.

An undertaker soon arrived to fit Mr. Hunt's body into a burial crate made of Douglas fir, a wood far more plentiful than pine in the Pacific Northwest. Mr. Combes consulted a doctor about his ear, but Emma had done all that could be done for it, other than give him a bottle of laudanum for pain. Gran's consumption settled back down. And a posse was sent out to join the others already searching for Harry Tracy.

Less than three weeks later, Harry lived up to his word once again. After being shot in the leg, he crawled into a field and killed himself with a bullet to the brain. Upon reading this news in the *Seattle Daily Times*, Emma wondered if he had gotten around to killing Cutter Lewis, or Lewis Cutter. And had the white willow bark helped him at all?

CHAPTER TWO

The Prescott Boarding House, Seattle
September, 1902

Emma lied by omission to Harry Tracy. It wasn't with malice; she was just comfortable with it. All three of the women at Prescott Boarding House knew how to tell great thumpers when the need arose.

Emma had, in fact, been married and divorced. She'd reclaimed Prescott as her name, but it had briefly been Byrne. Mrs. Ronan Byrne. Dark eyes, a mischievous smile, and a sweet tenor voice had captured her heart as Irishmen have captured women for years with those same tools. Soon enough, she found the prosperous young tavern owner was a drinker and violent when drunk. He opposed her keen attraction to the Seattle suffragettes.

"You daft girl," he said. "If women get the vote and keep a man from his drink, it puts paid to taverns like mine. Who'll take care of you then?"

When she joined the women anyway, he beat her. The second time, he beat her again and threw her out of their home above the tavern. Emma was a castaway.

To purchase freedom, she hadn't gone to one of the divorce mill states like Utah or the Dakotas. She could prove abuse and abandonment, and was pretty sure of adultery; Ronan did not oppose her, and the divorce was finalized after a waiting period of a year.

Emma had only lived with Ronan for six months when she was sixteen. Now eighteen, she thought she was over him, that her brain had finally crushed him out of her heart. It was simply easier to disavow his existence than explain it all over again whenever anyone asked. So she lied to Harry, claiming to be single and nothing more.

Her job depended on her discretion. After moving back to the boarding house, she began to teach in a school where her friend Lillian Stiltner taught (not that the school knew they had two such viperous women in their midst as a divorcee and a suffragette). The school contract specified Emma could neither marry nor keep the company of men. Emma believed that what the school didn't know of her former husband—or about the male boarders in her home, for that matter—was none of their business. However, she toed the line, more or less. She didn't smoke, or ride in a carriage with a man who was not a relative. She didn't drink (the occasional festive sherry was also none of her employer's howdy-do), and she wore dresses that reached to two inches above the heels of her shoes. Emma swept the classroom and cleaned the blackboards at least once a day. Like her mother and grandmother, she was efficient, accomplished, and showed signs of a stern nature; the students were cautious with her, but the school board loved her.

Three months had passed since Emma had received the gold from Harry Tracy. Until now, she'd kept it secret on the off-chance her mother might make her give it to the authorities. Emma was of the opinion that the authorities would no doubt find their own use for it, so she might as well keep it.

When her contract with the school came to an end, she turned in her notice, and finally told Gran and Ma what her real desire was. Gran put a hand to her chest, a lace hankie never far from her mouth lest she cough. "I want you to be what you want to be, Emma. But a healer? It is not likely to happen. Learn a trade, open a shop, become a dresser of hair. A woman can live well with that. If you need to doctor, you just take care of your mother and me, my girl."

"College? You want to go to college in Missouri?" Ma said when Gran had had her say.

"I must travel that far to study eclectic medicine."

"Eclectic medicine? What might that be, my girl?"

"I don't wish to study the bloodletting, blistering, and mercury purges of regular medicine. I believe in the restorative power of native flowers, greens, and herbs. This Missouri school accepts females as students. They teach the knowledge gleaned by the Red Man and other healers through the years. They offer pharmacy and surgery as well, but it's physiomedicine that interests me. I will be licensed in that."

"Your interest in botanicals is about to become a profession, is it?" Her mother sipped a bit of chamomile tea. A deeper V appeared between her brows, indicating that cogs were working inside. She pursed her lips, in and out.

Emma realized most mothers would say no. But her mother? She'd named her daughter Emma Sue in honor of Susan B. Anthony. Minerva taught Emma that a female must be tough not to fold under the dictates of society. Independence didn't come easy. Still, it was a lot to ask, crossing half a country on her own. Emma twisted a lock of hair that often escaped her chignon and stuffed it back in place.

Ma finally spoke. "Gran is right. Practicing a feminine skill is safer. Wiser. Keeping a shop or working as a nanny. An overeducated woman is an undesirable woman to most men. But, you are not likely to attract another man." Ma never mentioned Ronan's name, after having pronounced him dead to her when the divorce was finalized. Now she gave a shrug to her heavy shoulders. "A solitary occupation may suit you as it has me ever since your father died. How will we pay for this schooling?"

Emma leapt up to give a hug, an intimacy that startled her mother as well as herself. Gestures of affection were rare in the Prescott household. Emma recovered herself and sat back down, saying, "I have now saved enough for my living expenses. And there is more to tell about what I have hidden away."

Harry Tracy had given her the gold nuggets, telling her to wait at least two months to use them; she'd waited three. She showed them to Gran and her mother now. A trip to the assay office with a few of the nuggets had netted enough cash for tuition to the Eclectic Medical University in Kansas City.

The next month, Emma said goodbye to her family and her suffragette friend, Lillian, then moved to Kansas City. There she completed three sixteen-week terms with lectures and demonstrations four days a week, enough for a license in eclectic medicine. Dr. Emma Prescott would have gone on for advanced studies but for the Western Union telegram she received from Mr. Hardinger, their longtime boarder.

Seattle, Washington 6:15 pm December 28, 1903

Emma Prescott: Come at once. Mother and grandmother found murdered in boarding house. We are bereaved. Awaiting your arrival. Mr. Silas Hardinger.

* * *

No herbal or flower potion could assuage Emma's pain. She would even consider bloodletting if it could soothe her tortured heart. In a haze of shock, she took the train home to Seattle, then a carriage to Prescott Boarding House.

Emma arrived four days after she received the devastating telegram from Mr. Hardinger; she'd sent one back to him to let him know when she would reach her destination.

Mr. Hardinger and a stranger met her on the wooden veranda of the Prescott Boarding House on First Hill. It was a wide wraparound porch, typical of the Victorian style in the neighborhood, and it was much used in the summer by the family and boarders alike to catch the breezes from Puget Sound. Now it was wintery cold with a whistling wind, and there was no family but her. No boarders either, she learned as Mr. Hardinger explained, "I cannot stay here now that you will be alone in the house. It is not appropriate. Mr. Combes has departed as well. I am most sorry, Miss Prescott."

Emma's brain was like an out-of-tune piano; it was functioning but not with harmony. She didn't think to ask the men in, so they stood there in the Seattle freeze, Emma still clutching her travel carpetbag.

The man with Mr. Hardinger, a lawman as it turned out, added, "You cannot stay here alone either, not until Cutter has been apprehended."

That shocked Emma into speech. "Cutter? Cutter Lewis or Lewis Cutter? But how do you know it was him?"

"Goodwyn Lewis, Miss," the lawman clarified. "Although Cutter is a more accurate handle for the rogue."

"I saw him come down the porch steps as I came home from my office," Mr. Hardinger told her. "It was near dark, but I recognized the blighter, having made his acquaintance before when he tied me to a joist in the cellar. I hurried into the house, and that is when I found your dear mother and grandmother. In the parlor." He inhaled a deep breath then exhaled a puff that froze in the cold air. "Both had gone to meet their Maker."

The lawman said, "We don't know if he'll come back for you, you see. I doubt it, but I don't know why he came back here at all. Deputies will watch the house for you tonight until you find other accommodation on the morrow."

Emma asked about Ma and Gran. "The bodies. Are they still...?" She stopped, or she would sob.

The sheriff lowered his head, as if to contemplate mud on his boots. Apparently he was unable to meet the grief in her eyes any longer. "They've been buried, Miss. It is as well you did not see the condition in which Cutter left them."

Her logic told her that the bodies could not have waited all the days it took her to get there. But her emotions screamed how dare they deprive her of one last goodbye to Gran and Ma. All she said was, "You are sure Mr. Lewis did this deed?"

"Well, no, Miss. But he escaped the Oregon Penitentiary. Been there nearly since the day he last paid a visit to your boarding house. Appears he stole horses along the way and came right here. Do you know why he would return?"

Maybe it was the haze she was in. Maybe a lie was easier than the truth. "No, sir," she said without equivocation. "I have no idea." Then she followed up with a truth. "I thought he might be dead, that Mr. Tracy might have killed him before he killed himself."

"No. Cutter was run down by a posse that Tracy outran."

The lawman and Mr. Hardinger finally left, and Emma entered the boarding house. Never before had it seemed so quiet. All she heard was the grandfather clock, its tick slow now that no one had wound it for days. She smelled dampness. In the Northwest, an untended house could mildew in no time. Emma shook her head, trying to clear it, to keep on track.

She finally set her carpetbag down, removed her travel cape, hat, and gloves, leaving them on the hall tree. Then she ventured into the parlor. Blood was still on the ornate chairs. From the bubble of pain that encased her, a thought emerged. *I must get after that stain. Ma hates a mess in this room.* Her brain struggled to overcome grief.

Let's see. Let's see. Yes! The gold. He wanted the gold. Tracy hadn't killed him, and Cutter guessed he left it here. What else could it be?

She felt no fear for her welfare, but knew that she probably should. Emma was too overwhelmed with other emotions for an additional one to lay claim. At the parlor desk, she felt for the folder in its pigeon-hole and pulled it out. The buckskin bag was right there. She emptied it onto the desktop. Nuggets and flakes of gold spilled out. The only ones missing were those she'd spent on college.

So Cutter left without them. Why?

To keep from falling, she sat on the desk chair. Her sluggish head finally dredged up the answer. She'd never told Ma and Gran where she put the bag of nuggets; neither had asked to know. They'd considered it her gift from Tracy. If they had known the location, they could have given the gold to Cutter. Maybe it would have saved their lives.

I am to blame for their deaths!

Slowly Emma stood and worked her way to her own room where she curled on her narrow bed. She removed her glasses and wept deeply, glad to be alone. She did not move, not even to respond to a knock she heard on the front door in the late afternoon. *Must be the deputies arriving or someone paying their respects.* She needed to talk to neither. She needed to plan.

CHAPTER THREE

The Prescott Boarding House, Seattle
January 5, 1904

The next morning, a sleepless Emma left the house with a small lump of gold, one the size of a black tab of Sen-Sen breath freshener. She wrapped it in a hanky and tucked it into her glove, then walked from First Hill down the street, churned to mud by feet, hooves, and wheels in the icy rain. On her way to Pioneer Square, she was careful not to step on the glass blocks in the street that allowed light to the underground. The noise and smell of the city center nearly overpowered her as she stopped before a tavern called Irish Rose. It was darkened this early in the day. Her eyes raised to the windows above, the place that had once been her home when she lived as the wife of Ronan Byrne. Curtains were all drawn, and she saw no sign of light.

She was afraid. Her mother commanded in her head, "Whether you feel fearful or not, your first mission is to create safety for yourself." It appeared that, dead or alive, her mother was in control. Otherwise, Emma might never have returned to this place and its bittersweet memories. With an intake of breath and a literal squaring of her shoulders, Emma pulled out a key and opened the tavern door. Ronan had never asked for it back.

She did not enter the main room of the tavern but turned toward the staircase on the right. It curled to a second floor. Here she walked down a creaky hall, then knocked on the door at the end, at first softly then with more force. Finally, she banged with her fist.

"Thunderation!" She heard him yell through the door. As it flew open, he continued with "What damn zounderkite knocks at this time of..."

His words trailed off as he saw her there in the dim light, shivering with cold. He was nude to the chest, clothed only in long johns below. His dark hair was a wild mass of curls, and his beautiful eyes were now red and puffy.

"Hello, husband," she said, with no small amount of acid. Emma felt the resolve her mother displayed in messy situations. Ma's presence lent her fortitude.

Ronan hacked a whisky cough as he stared. Then he said, "No longer a husband by your own choice. You didn't come home then. Why are you here now?"

For the first time, Emma considered he might have been playing a game back then, hoping to see her plead with him to take her back. How could he know her so little?

She passed by him into the living room that had been hers, went to a window, and threw back a curtain. "I'm here to hire help that I shall pay for."

Ronan sat on the sofa, legs splayed, making no effort to dress himself. As he began to roll a smoke, he said, "So this is business, not personal? Then state your request of me."

"My grandmother and mother are dead."

He had the decency to look surprised but the temerity to add, "Didn't think anything would take down that battle-axe mother of yours."

"A knife did the job with no difficulty." Emma explained the deaths to Ronan, stopping short of how she came by gold.

But finances were definitely on his mind. "Did they leave you well-feathered?" he asked. "Have you inherited money then?"

She ignored that and said, "I need two men to guard the boarding house for a short time until I can arrange other plans. Two of your bouncers, perhaps, or other men you believe I can trust. Men who will keep me safe if the blackguard returns with his knife. I will pay you for this courtesy. You pay them as much of the amount as you feel they are worth."

"If you have come into money, my girl, remember I am your husband..."

"As you hastened to point out, *was* my husband. You have no claim on anything of mine. Isn't divorce a wonderful state of affairs? Aren't you glad you did not oppose such a dissolution of contract?" She removed the hanky from her glove. "What I have is this one nugget, more than enough to pay for this request."

As she unwrapped the gold from her hanky, a half-dressed woman peeked out from the bedroom to see who was in the living room. Emma believed she recognized the girl as one of the waitresses at Ronan's tavern, the Irish Rose below this floor. If asked, Emma would deny the shiver of jealousy.

She stood. "I expect the first man to arrive at noon today and to be replaced by another at midnight tonight. If I need them for more than a week, I will agree to lengthened terms."

Ronan smiled, and she still found it warmed her heart, at least until he stood, stretched, scratched himself, and said, "Then away with you and await my man. I now have another bird to pluck in my bed."

Emma slipped out the apartment door as Ronan went in the bedroom door.

* * *

On her walk home, Emma stopped at a butcher, a green grocer, and a bakery, ordering foods to be delivered. By the time she arrived at Prescott Boarding House mid-day, a questionable-looking thug raised eyebrows in the homes of First Hill, as he swung up the street, whistling a ballad.

"Are you sure we should leave you with him, Miss?" asked one of the deputies watching the house, awaiting the man who would replace them. "I've come across Irishman like him before. Seems a rowdy specimen to me."

He was a great bull of a man, nearly as wide as tall, not young but still on the better side of forty. A red flannel shirt stretched to capacity over his arms. On a finger he held a jacket over his back. His mustache, the size of a Fuller brush, hid much of his lower face.

"Yes, I am sure. I will be fine." Emma had gone to Ronan for tough guys so she must not quail when one arrived. She noticed the speed with which the deputies left.

When the Irishman climbed the porch, she could see that the mustache tried to hide a scar that crossed from cheek to cheek.

Oh dear. He must be tough to survive whatever happened there.

The Irishman bowed. "Ronan sent me. You are Mrs. Byrne?"

"Yes. No. Well, I mean I am called Miss Prescott now."

The man smiled, but did not quite laugh. He said, "Now you and I both know who you are. I am Timothy Crogan, come to save you from whatever you need saving from."

She explained the deaths of her family and her return from Kansas City. Then she ended with, "I expect you to repel the rapscallion that haunts me here, Mr. Crogan. You and a compatriot will keep me alive until I can plan my next steps." She needed time to decide whether to stay or, if she left, to where.

Timothy listened. He was taller than Emma, although he was still standing on a step below porch level. "I'm happy to, as long as there's no more of this 'Mr. Crogan' cow-slaver. Call me Timothy, my girl. Now describe the scoundrel, if you will."

She did her best, but realized she had been so focused on Harry Tracy that her memory of Cutter was foggy. Her clearest recollection was actually of his knife. "Well, he carries a hunting knife. And his name is Goodwyn Lewis. Cutter is merely a nickname, I believe."

"I doubt Mother Lewis named him that. A nickname, we will agree."

"The knife is enormous; you should keep that well in mind."

"But the lad himself. How did he look?"

I'd say mid-twenties...um, under six feet. Appeared fit enough. Ate a great deal. Cutty-eyed, you know, sneaky-like. And a sneer."

Timothy nodded. "If I see a sneaky-eyed, sneering gent approach with an enormous nose picker, I'll surely thump him for you."

"Are you making fun of me, Timothy?"

"Nothing of the sort, Miss Prescott. Now show me the other entrances to the house."

"There is but one more, other than windows, of course." She led him through the house, down the back stairs to the cellar and an exit to the yard.

"We shall block this one."

"That won't do, Timothy."

"Are you telling me my job, Miss Prescott?"

"I'm telling you it is the route to the privy."

"Ah. Well then, we'll block it but only in the night."

* * *

With Timothy guarding the house from the veranda, Emma thought about food. Her orders of provisions had not been delivered yet, and she found she was not hungry anyway. Instead of eating, she went to the parlor. The room told the tale of a battle. She scrubbed the blood from Gran and Ma off the furniture, straightened the disarrayed chairs, upturned spilled vases and restored stacks of magazines. She picked up the fire poker to return it to its stand, gasping when she saw dry blood and dark hair in a sticky lump on its end.

Cutter's?

She hoped her mother got in a good lick or two before she succumbed to the bastard. It would be no surprise to Emma if she had, but it might have come as one to Goodwyn Lewis. Her mother's resolve had accompanied her that morning when she visited her ex-husband. Emma could not imagine being without her. Minerva had taught her to be strong, in control of her future as much as a female could be. But Emma felt broken now, in need of her mother's drive. She hoped the visitation would happen again and soon.

Help me, Ma.

Emma went to the kitchen when the baker's boy arrived with loaves. The rich aroma of the still-warm bread ignited a hunger pang and convinced her she must eat. She found butter, eggs and cheese in the larder. A dry storage pantry was filled with fruit preserves put up by Gran and Ma, plus Mason jars of watermelon pickles, sauerkraut, beans, corn, and peas. Emma wouldn't starve.

Thanks for the help, Ma. The thought brought a wry smile to her face.

When she had eaten, she took two slabs of bread, each slathered with butter and raspberry rhubarb preserves, out to Timothy Crogan. He was sitting on the porch, jacket on with its collar turned up, his eyes toward the street.

Emma set the plate of bread and a mug of coffee on the small porch table. "A bit of repast. Sorry it isn't more. Most supplies have not yet arrived."

"Ah, lass, it's far more than asked." He actually doffed his flat cap to her. She saw that his head did not have the luxurious crop of hair that his mustache promised it might. *How old is he?* Her first guess of close to forty might have been a bit too high. The creases around his eyes could be from hard living more than age. "Are you comfortable, Timothy? Do you need a rug for warmth?"

"I am bright-eyed and bushy-tailed, Miss Prescott."

"Good. Then I shall sleep now. It is some time since I have, and I would prefer not to worry about being knifed."

"The knife would have to get through me to get to you. And I am far too big for that. You are safe."

She believed him, and the tenseness in her neck eased the tiniest bit. "Thank you. Please do not frighten the grocer's boy when he delivers."

It was still the pallid daylight of a winter afternoon, but she ached with exhaustion. She went to her room, closed the curtains on the bay window that overlooked the street, put on a nightgown, and slept until early morning.

When she replaced her spectacles and came downstairs to look outside, she saw a different man on the porch, smaller than Timothy and older. She also saw the pistol stuck in his britches, and a baseball bat resting against the veranda's railing. The changing of the guard had happened in the night without her notice.

She prepared herself for a visit to her mother's old friend, Louella Braxton. On her way out the door, she offered the new man a cup of coffee and found out his name was Allen. That is all he said. *He is certainly not the jovial soul that Timothy seems to be,* she thought as she headed up the street, glad of her winter cape. The ruts in the road were beginning to freeze, and the streetcars seemed to squeal more than usual.

Louella Braxton was a stalwart muck-a-muck in the suffragette movement, a movement important to the Prescott women for three generations. Gran had met suffragettes when she was a Mercer girl, one of the young women brought to Seattle forty years before by Asa Mercer, local entrepreneur. He'd traveled East to bring brides back to Seattle, from places like the workhouses of Massachusetts. White women were needed to marry the pioneer lumbermen and sailing tycoons. The man Gran married revered her and took care of her with the pride he might endow on a prized heifer. Emma never knew her grandfather, but it was not a bad life, Gran always said.

Emma's Ma, Minerva, was the only one of Gran's many children who lived into adulthood. She inherited her mother's streak of independence, supporting the suffragettes as well. She'd married, but Mr. Prescott died years ago in a woodland accident. Some said it was not such a tragedy, since he would have died soon enough from Minerva's sharp tongue and bullheaded nature. Emma knew that notion was tommy-rot, that her father had been a dreamer, more at home illustrating plants than cutting them down. Minerva ruled because Minerva had to. After his death, Ma took to running their home as a boarding house like peas take to soup. The boarders found good food, clean rooms, and pleasant company.

These memories of Gran and Ma accompanied Emma to the door of the Braxton home which had none of the sillier Victorian frills of her own boarding house. The American

Craftsman was square, squat, and utilitarian. It was well-suited to the lady of the house. Mrs. Braxton invited Emma in, took her to a front-room-cum-office which was overfilled with desks and bookcases. A young woman there looked up from stamping a pile of postcards and gasped, "Emma!"

"Lillian, I hoped to see you!" The two hugged, cheek by cheek. When they separated, Emma explained to Mrs. Braxton, "Lillian Stiltner and I are friends, in fact, taught school together. I have not seen her since leaving for college."

"Perhaps, Lillian, you could bring us tea," said Mrs. Braxton, putting a pointed end to their short reunion.

Lillian turned away, winked at Emma, and said, "Of course. I will come see you, Emma, very soon. You can tell me all then. About school...and your mother and..."

"Absolutely. So much to tell." For the first time since receiving the telegram from Mr. Hardinger, Emma felt cheered enough to smile at a friend.

Mrs. Braxton went on to express all the right commiseration, over sounds of women laughing from another room. Their chatter reminded Emma of the lodgings she had in Kansas City, a small hotel only for females. It was a lively place to be. *Was it only last week?*

Mrs. Braxton brought her to the sorrowful present. "Your mother and grandmother both gone in one afternoon. Such a loss to you. Such a loss to suffragettes. And a personal loss to me. I have known your mother all of my life."

"All those are reasons I am here," Emma said. "She trusted you, Mrs. Braxton. Now I must plan for my future, you see, and it may well involve you." She was surprised to see the pity in the face of her mother's old friend lose some of its warmth.

"What can I do?" Mrs. Braxton asked, cautious now.

Emma explained her plan, beginning with why she could not simply reopen the boarding house, at least not yet. Not until the murderer was apprehended. In case he was after her, too, which she doubted. "I have found a man to guard the house during the day. I am now a licensed practitioner of eclectic medicine, and I wish to open an office to begin my practice. I feel confident the boarding house is safe for such daytime activity."

"Well, I don't know," Mrs. Braxton said, an edge to her voice.

Emma carried on. "Even if the man called Goodwyn Lewis is still around, and there is no reason to think he is, and even if he is interested in me for some unknown reason, he would not come during daylight hours when the house is a hubbub of activity. He has no reason to bother others."

If Emma examined what she just said, she'd have to admit she was downplaying her own concerns with an overly bright outlook. She was saying too much, more than necessary to interest Mrs. Braxton in her idea. But once started, she could not stop. Words toppled out like pieces of gum from one of those new vending machines she'd seen in the train station. She explained that she would have plenty of room for suffragette activity. Looking around the crowded room, she emphasized there'd be ample area for several more desks, workers with typewriters, and even one of those new mimeography machines she'd read about. "Imagine hand-cranking your own bulletins," she enthused, selling her idea hard. "And you'd have your front room back."

In return for the office space, all Emma asked of the Braxton household was lodging for herself. "I would not need board, as I can use my own kitchen during the day. As could your suffragettes. I just need quiet quarters for the evenings and nights."

Mrs. Braxton's countenance puckered in what Emma took to be obstinacy. She looked like the pug dog Emma had once seen in Seattle's Chinatown. "My dear girl, that will never do. What if this outlaw is after you? You cannot go from your place to mine daily. He will follow you and, if not on the street, he will find you here. I cannot allow that, not only for your safety but the rest of the women who come and go here. No, I am sorry. You must abandon this city, leaving a trail for nobody. I see no other way. Your mother would say the same, God rest her dear soul."

Well!

On the trek home, Emma was vexed at the woman who gave lip service to help but no actual help when asked. In fairness, she realized she was irritated with herself. Of course, a plan like hers was riddled with holes. Her brain wasn't working. She had not the slightest notion of how to walk around undetected or to defend herself for that matter. "I am a featherbrain. I must think."

Like it or not, Mrs. Braxton was right. Cutter could be anywhere. That man over there in the top hat...the old one with a woman and child looking in the candy shop window. Emma had no clear memory of how he would appear if he cleaned himself up and sheathed the knife.

She was so deep in her own thoughts, head down against the misty rain, she did not see the two men until she climbed the steps to her porch. At the top, she saw them sitting with the table between them, Timothy Crogan with a gun in his lap. The other man was Mr. Combes.

"Oh!" she exclaimed. It came out as a squeak.

Timothy asked, "Is this Cutter, Miss? Caught him sniffing around."

"Oh!" she squeaked again before finding more words. "Dear me, no. Thank you, Timothy, but no! This is Mr. Combes, a former boarder here. He is not our scoundrel, I assure you." She added, "He is a dentist," as though that would matter.

Timothy Crogan's eyes twinkled. "Ah, well. He said as much, but I needed to be sure."

Combes touched his ear below his homburg where a piece of his lobe was missing. "I have my own reasons to avoid the disagreeable Cutter Lewis. I would happily shoot him myself if I were to see him again."

"Then we are allies. Sorry to be a wisenheimer, Mr. Combes. I'll just make a trip around the house, use the necessary, get out of your way." He hefted himself off the wicker chair, tucked the pistol under his coat, and swaggered down the steps.

They watched him go, then Emma took his chair on the veranda, saying, "I am so sorry if Timothy scared you."

"Well, he is rather an imposing fellow," said Mr. Combes, reseating himself. "But I am well pleased you have support of a hooligan like him to keep you safe."

"You understand convention dictates that I cannot invite you in, Mr. Combes. No matter how cold here on the porch."

"It is fine, Miss Prescott. I wanted to tell you how terrible I feel about your mother and your grandmother. They were so kind to me."

"Please. I believe it is time you call me Emma."

"And I am Otis."

Otis. What an awful name, she thought. *I prefer Mr. Combes.*

"I enjoyed living here for nearly two years. I feel I know you rather well, Emma."

"Yes, well, it has all turned topsy-turvy, hasn't it?" Emma was not as interested in Otis' problems as she was in solving her own. But there was no need to be unkind. "I will be happy to provide you with an excellent reference for another boarding house."

"But that is rather the problem. I am leaving town. I have an opportunity to take over a dentistry practice in Port Angeles, at the foot of the Olympic Mountains. To start a business of my own in Seattle is too costly for me. On the frontier, opportunity abounds. Patrons with the money for dentistry are moving west all the time for the lumbering and the shipping industries. A growing port to be sure."

He sounds excited, mirthful even, but what does this have to do with me? Emma wanted to give him a good tongue-wagging. Couldn't he see that as his fortunes were rising, hers were sinking to the root cellar? "It sounds delightful, Otis. It appears you will not need that reference."

"Emma, I don't want to go alone. I have long admired you and how you cared for my ear when I encountered Cutter. I know you cook and keep an orderly house. I find you a sensible girl. And a lovely one."

What on earth? Lovely, I am not.

"Would you agree to marry me, Emma, to move to Port Angeles for a fresh start?"

Emma felt her face make ridiculous changes. Her eyes widened, as did her nostrils and her mouth. Her cheeks began to burn. "I...but...you..."

"I know it's sudden, but circumstance has rushed my decision process. It does not leave time for a proper courtship."

She tried to listen but could not. It was a solution, moving so far away from Cutter and whatever he was up to. But she was divorced, and that made her second-hand goods. Otis, Mr. Combes, had no way to know that. She had no wish to reveal her secret. "I am so very flattered, Otis. But, I must say no. Definitely no."

His mirth collapsed as hope drained away. "You need not decide this moment but think..."

"No, the answer is no." Emma's heart took over from her head; she could not let him go thinking he was unworthy. "I have a secret, Otis, that I live with and which keeps me from your kind consideration. I trust you with it now. I am divorced from a man who often was cruel to me. My mother took me back to live here. This is why I am no marriage prospect for you."

She felt humiliated. A woman so unworthy of a man that he had to thrash her? Otis would believe that it was her fault her husband reviled her in such a way.

But Otis surprised her. He did not appear to think that at all. "Oh, Emma. I am so sorry that any man would treat a woman like you in such a manner. It is too regretful for me, for us both, that we cannot build a kinder future together. I would consider becoming your second husband. Would you consider it?"

Emma felt uplifted by this gentleman. Men had not been high on her list recently. But now was no time to think of it further. No. Definitely not the time.

She reached out her gloved hand to hold his for a moment and thanked him sincerely but did not change her mind. Otis departed soon after, there being very little left for the two of them to say but to wish each other great success.

Emma might have cried had Timothy Crogan not appeared instantly to replace Otis on the porch. "So the Combes lad was making his move, was he?"

"Timothy! Mr. Crogan! What a thing to say! And were you eavesdropping?"

"I have little leeway to guard you without overhearing you, Miss Prescott."

"Otis is a sincere gentleman, I am sure as eggs is eggs of that. Do you think me so unworthy of catching a good man's eye?" She was upset and taking it out on him. Her mother, still in her head, gave her permission to act badly.

"No miss, not in the least. An altogether attractive young lady you are. I am saddened to hear what a bounder your husband proved to be. I might not have taken his employment had I known, but then I would not have met you to care about it."

"Well, now you know. I'm sure it will make great amusement for you to share with the boys at the Irish Rose tonight." She stood, affected the rigid spine of her mother, and marched into the house.

The butcher had delivered, so Emma went to the kitchen to cut up a chicken. Everything was wrong. Ma and Gran were dead, and she was all alone. Emma cried as she amputated a wing.

Worse than that, she was responsible. She had hidden the gold. Maybe she deserved to die in order to pay for their deaths. Wham! went the butcher knife, removing thigh from leg.

Mrs. Braxton was no help. And Emma couldn't marry Otis, and who knew when she'd ever be able to start her medical practice?

Chicken pieces tumbled into the pot of boiling water.

Her tantrum fizzled in time. It wasn't in her nature to sit on the pity pot too long. She couldn't stay mad at Timothy Crogan, either. He was the only person she had to talk with. Besides, she needed his help. So she did what women do by way of asking forgiveness: when the meal was ready, she invited him to eat.

"Come inside, Timothy," she said. "The neighbors may talk, but it is too cold for a man to eat his midday meal on the porch. And I certainly won't eat mine out here. So the neighbors will just have to flap their gums."

His surprise at the invitation was obvious from his raised eyebrows, but the mustache nearly hid his smile along with the scar across his face. As they shared the comfort of chicken and dumplings, Emma told him about her visit to Louella Braxton. "She feels I must move to a new place, one unknown to Goodwyn Lewis. Or to me, for that matter."

"She is correct," he said as he held his plate for a second serving.

"But this is my home, where I want to set up my medical practice, where all my memories reside. I do not want to be run off by an unprincipled rogue."

"Then, Miss Prescott, we must put this man Cutter to bed with a shovel." He shrugged then popped the last dumpling into his mouth.

The comment stopped her rant. She paled and bridled at the thought. "I don't intend either you or I should commit murder. I merely wish to live here while avoiding the graveyard myself."

He lifted four fingers as he counted off. "We kill him, or you clear off, or he clears off and you'll live in fear forever, or he kills you. You are on the horns of a dilemma."

"Indeed, I am." She took her napkin from her lap and slapped it onto the table. Emma needed to enter a world she understood, one that didn't feel like quicksand under her feet. She wanted to be among the botanicals in which she had faith to soothe, heal and calm. "I will consider it later. At the moment, I wish to visit the apothecary. I want to begin my practice. I must purchase additional stock."

"I suggest I accompany you, Miss Prescott. Allen has arrived for his watch here at the house."

"You think I am not safe on city streets, amid crowds, then. Maybe Cutter is long gone, and all this worry is worthless."

Timothy stared at her for a moment. "Here is what I think: you know exactly what this man wants, he won't stop until he gets it, and you are experiencing the pipe dream of an opium disciple if you think he will simply go away. So yes, Miss Prescott. I think you are unsafe on city streets or anywhere on your own."

CHAPTER FOUR

The Prescott Boarding House, Seattle
January 6, 1904

Emma possessed an admirable deadpan. Her hazel
eyes sometimes twinkled or her lips trembled when flooded
with emotion, but she had learned to keep her feelings more
or less to herself. Since she was neither a raving beauty nor
a warty horn toad, she doubted others noticed her at all.
Maybe your countenance was only animated if you were
the type who was sure people were looking at you.

But Timothy Crogan had read her like a book. She
looked at him, mouth agape, as they walked together down
the street toward the shopping district. *You know exactly
what this man wants.* That's what he'd said. Either she'd
revealed herself in some manner, or Timothy was some
kind of wizard. She'd never told him about Tracy's gold, but
he knew something kept Cutter sniffing around. How much
else did the Irishman intuit? Could she trust him fully? He
seemed to want to protect her.

Timothy looked at her sideways. "I seem to have
startled you, Miss Prescott, at least considering your jaw has
dropped nearly to your knees."

She snapped her yap shut.

"I admire how bravely you handle your fear and grief.
I know men who would buckle at less. It is an honor to look

after you, on the street as well as at your home. I feel I stand in for a father that way, ready to fight for you."

Well, doesn't that beat the devil. Emma was so surprised, she felt the need to babble. She may have learned to hide emotion in her face, but it often burst forth in the form of chatter. When nervous, she prattled. Like now.

"You shall find the day interesting, I believe, Timothy. There is much that can be done with natural concoctions, used judiciously. That is the point of eclectic medicine. Seek relief through nature, and only rely on pharmaceuticals or surgery when you must. All forms of cures must be considered."

He nodded but looked away, this way and that.

Emma continued. "I do not trust patent medicines. They create more slaves to dependency. Packaged elixirs and tonics? Mostly morphine, saltpeter, mercury, alcohol. Cure you by killing you first," she scoffed as they strolled side by side.

She had long created her own botanicals by purchasing fresh flora at the wholesalers in warehouses on Western Avenue. She even ventured to an herbalist in Chinatown. Her favorite way to build her stock was to glean specimens from the forests that surrounded Seattle. Emma harvested and dried the seeds, bark, and leaves at home. "Purity is key, Timothy. I would like to process more, but fresh stock is unavailable in January."

On this sojourn, she hoped to increase her supply of the medical apparatus and gadgetry that she'd studied at Eclectic Medical University in Kansas City. She knew the immediate future was up in the air until the Cutter state of affairs was dealt with. She could hardly open a clinic knowing a devil might break in. *Has he disappeared for good? Is he out there? Will the sheriff run him to ground? Ah well.*

Emma put her concerns aside for the moment, and allowed herself to be chirky with delight. She could not keep silent.

"My plan is to start small, to go to patients' homes to support me as I build Dr. Emma's Eclectic Medicine in the boarding house. I need more stoppered bottles, powder tins, mortars and pestles, eye cups, and, well, so much else. Plus a medical bag, a fine leather one I will use for years. I know there are modern chemists, but I prefer the apothecary down here. His spices are the best in the city."

As they turned down a passage no wider than an alley, Emma wasn't sure Timothy listened to her at all. His eyes swept the crowds on the main street, then the few pedestrians after their turn into the narrow side street. She asked, "When in guard mode, do your ears not work, Timothy? Can you not speak when using your eyes so?"

"I am aware of a little bird chattering constantly, Miss Prescott. But my attention is engaged elsewhere."

Two bright show globes, one blue and the other red, glowed in the apothecary window, reflecting the bright sun that pierced the wintry afternoon. As Emma and the shop owner discussed arcane liniments, lozenges, suppositories, atomizers, and powders, Timothy watched the door.

"What a restorative activity! I am more eager than ever to move forward with my career." Emma beamed as she handed her packages to Timothy.

"I am now more pack mule than guardian," he protested, passing through the door to exit the shop.

The knife hit his chest before the door closed. It knocked him into the glass display bay window, but he maintained his footing. Medical supplies scattered across the floor inside and out to the street, all except one tight-wrapped bolt of cotton gauze. It was pinned to his chest by the knife. Both bandage and blade teetered momentarily before, as one, they thudded heavily to the ground.

After one stunned moment, Timothy yelled, "Get inside!" and pushed Emma back into the store. He slammed the door and thundered away down the narrow street.

Emma stared open-mouthed at the enormous knife, now harmless among her supplies on the apothecary hardwood floor. It was enmeshed in the bolt of gauze she'd intended to cut into strips for non-adherent wound care. "Miserable bye-blow," she swore, having never called anyone a bastard aloud before. Then she bolted like a she-wolf, following the Irishman around the corner and onto the main thoroughfare.

There she stopped, furious tears hazing her sight. Dozens of people dashed around streetcars and carriages, confusing her in the dazzling sun. She had no idea which way Timothy had gone. "Damnation," she swore, to the surprise of a portly passerby who continued on a little faster.

Soon, Timothy zigzagged back through the crowd, a look of disgust on his face. "Lost him," he scowled. "But we now know for a fact he is after you and willing to go through me."

Emma fingered the jagged tear on the front of his jacket. The knife had stopped there, leaving his chest unharmed. She saw no sign of blood. "The gauze saved your life. That fierce blade became entangled in the mesh, lost speed, and died with only the power to slice through your frock coat."

"So that explains it. Wondered why I was still alive and kicking."

"I will mend this," was all she could say by way of thanking him. Then she began to tremble.

"You are shaken, Miss Prescott. Let's return to the apothecary and sit for a moment."

She drew a great breath and hissed out the words. "I am shaken, Timothy. But not with fear. With absolute fury.

Such a pigeon-livered bounder to attack from afar. And you an innocent man. I become more and more convinced the world would be better without this mongrel."

Timothy smiled at her. "I don't believe anyone has afore called me an innocent man."

They returned to the apothecary to retrieve her purchases. The shopkeeper had gathered her things together, rewrapped the packages and tied them with string. "I have included a new bolt of gauze," he said to Emma, patting her hand. He'd also rounded up a patrolman who took their names and descriptions of the incident.

"That will come to naught," Timothy said as they left the shop once more. "I never even saw the man other than a flash of a brown coat and hat."

"But we know who he is." Emma said. "And it appears I now have a weapon of my own."

"What weapon is that, Miss Prescott?"

"The shopkeeper also packaged up Cutter's knife."

For the rest of the walk home, Emma was silent. She did not feel the need to prattle. Instead, behind her deadpan countenance, she was considering her next steps.

* * *

At the boarding house, Emma's suffragette friend awaited her on the veranda. Lillian Stiltner was a round package of cuteness in a blue wool nip-waisted coat with a fur muff on her hands. She was past her prime, maybe even in her thirties, but still had the sweet face of a baby doll. Her cheeks were blushed from the chill, and irrepressible blonde curls escaped from her wool cloche.

"Mr. Allen said you would not be long, and here you are," Lillian exclaimed with pleasure.

"I am very happy to see you, Lillian. Please go inside where it is warm. Maybe put a kettle on. I will join you shortly." Emma turned to Timothy. "I have one more request of you before you leave this evening."

His eyes were following Lillian into the house as he said, "I will not be leaving this evening. Allen and I will both keep watch tonight."

"Ah. Well then, if you could do me this kindness, I will have dinner for you when you return."

"Agreed, Miss Prescott."

She reached in her purse and extracted a ten dollar banknote. She would not have trusted him with such a thing just a day ago. Now he seemed an old friend. "Will you go to the ticket office of the Puget Sound Navigation Company and book me passage on the SS *Clallam*, a vessel heading for Victoria two mornings from now, on January 8?"

If he was surprised he did not show it. "Shall I use your real name?"

"Perhaps they will not demand a name, but if they do, make one up. A boy's name, I think. But nothing awful. Not Clyde or Beauregard or Hezekiah. It is no time for a sense of humor, sir."

While Timothy was away, Emma shared the kitchen with Lillian. One peeled potatoes, and the other folded biscuit batter in an old wooden bowl. While they worked, they drank from mugs of dark, sugared tea. Its soothing power helped Emma explain her dilemma to her friend.

"I do not think the Cutter villain will go away. I am afraid he will get to me one way or another, and that means Timothy will be hurt. Or killed. I certainly can't allow a thing like that."

"But why, Emma? Why is this outlaw so interested in you?"

As Emma explained about the gold, she placed the biscuit batter onto a buttered pan. "He believes the gold is still here. And he is right. What is left of it."

"You didn't deposit it?"

"No. Tracy warned me to keep still about it. I didn't want to be questioned about its provenance. If Ma had revealed its location to him, maybe this would not have happened." Her voice cracked.

Lillian huffed. "A madman stalking your family? Emma, you are not to blame."

"Maybe not. But I alone can fix it. If I leave here, he will surely assume I have taken it with me. That's the only way to assure the boarding house is safe from him."

"Could you convert it to banknotes?"

"I can do that in Canada. Fewer questions will be asked." She sighed heavily as she placed the biscuits into the oven. "If he catches me with the gold before that time, he will have no reason to come back here."

Lillian set down the potato knife and dried her hands. She hugged her friend. "I am afraid for you, Emma. Life is out of control."

The touch of a friend warmed Emma to her soul. Then she pulled away and sent Lillian on an errand back to her own home. "Please do not wear your hat. Let your yellow hair show. If my watcher is out there, I don't want him to think you are me. When you and Timothy return, I'll explain to you both what I am preparing to do."

* * *

Goodwyn 'Cutter' Lewis was at that moment spying on the boarding house from a room he'd let, on a short term basis, in lodgings across the street. Its view was limited in that he could only see the front door of the Prescott

Boarding House, but having tried twice to enter through the back, he was aware they now kept that door locked.

He'd returned to his lodgings after the fiasco with the big Irishman, a plan that had cost him his best frigging blade. Why in damnation had it failed him? He noticed the other mick, Allen, had arrived to guard the house at night, and he'd seen a blonde woman over there through a window. She appeared to be a pretty thing, one he'd like to inspect at closer range.

Through the dust-flocked curtains on his window, he observed Timothy Crogan leave almost immediately after he and the Prescott woman returned home that day. What the hell was that about? He saw no sign of a wound. Was the Irishman made of iron?

Cutter decided to follow. Maybe he was only going off duty, to booze with other potato heads. But maybe his trip would be more interesting. And, if Cutter got the chance, he'd try again to gut that sumbitch.

Cutter dogged Crogan down Mill Street to Pier Number One. The port was alive with noise, vermin, and the stench of rotting wood, fish, and livestock. He nearly lost his prey in the crowds of passengers as they braided their way between dockers and stevedores who were offloading and onloading ships. The hordes were in his favor, hiding his presence from the Irishman.

To his surprise, his quarry stopped at the ticket office of the Puget Sound Navigation Company. When Crogan departed, it took Cutter very little time to pressure information from the PSNC clerk. The Irishman had purchased a ticket on the January 8 sailing of the SS *Clallam*.

Now don't that just wake snakes, he thought as he bought a ticket for the same steamer. *If the Prescott woman's leaving town, she's damn sure taking the gold with her.* He was very proud of himself for managing such complex logic all on his own. That bastard Harry Tracy had never given him enough credit, damn the man. All this bother could have been avoided if Tracy had entrusted him instead of a four-eyed woman with no claim whatsoever on his wealth.

* * *

When Timothy and Lillian both returned from their errands, they ate with Emma in the kitchen. Allen, on watch, was given a thick slab of beef, gravy, and buttered potatoes.

"I've come up with a plan, Timothy, and I would like to explain it to both you and Lillian." Emma passed her Gran's antique gravy boat, the one the old lady had called her saucier.

"I'm pleased to know you have a plan," Timothy said. "I presume it involves shipping a boy across international waters to Canada in two days' time?"

"Yes!" Lillian grinned at Timothy, then added, "Now I get it. A boy who will be wearing my younger brother's clothing!"

Emma rolled her eyes, a gesture that her blue steel-rimmed glasses enlarged. "You are both first rate Pinkertons. I leave for Canada the day after tomorrow, dressed as a boy. Goodwyn Lewis will have a very hard time identifying me, even if he is watching the house. I'll look like just another delivery boy to him."

Timothy set down his fork. "You mean to sail away from my protection? To another country? What do you know of Canada?" He sounded ready to pull back on the reins.

Lillian appeared worried as well. "It is very large and unsettled, I have been told. Filled with bears and bad men."

"I am fairly certain Miss Prescott now has a knife that will handle bears and ratbags, Miss Stiltner, if you'll pardon an Irishman's French." He smiled at her, his mustache covering the scar at his mouth.

Lillian giggled.

Emma wondered if it was merely a nervous laughter. *Or is Lillian flirting?* Certainly, her own nerves felt tingly with stress. "Pay no attention to such nonsense, Lillian. Ma and I visited Victoria once, spending two nights before our return. It is very up-to-date, you know. I do not need to concern myself with the rest of that wild country for the moment." She turned to Timothy. "And I am not sailing away from your protection. I need you here for at least the next two days and nights to stand guard. It grieves me to request that you risk your life, now that we know the Cutter villain is still off the leash and running free."

"This is my job. Once on the vessel, you should be safe. I will not relax until then. Be not concerned in the least."

Emma felt suddenly somber. "It may be a long time before I return. In fact, if Victoria suits me, I may not return. I have no family, no holds here anymore... except you two, my old and my new friends." Emma felt her eyes spill a bit of liquid, and she stopped for a swig of tea.

Her friends turned their attention to their plates and passed dishes to each other, giving Emma time.

When she could control her voice, she continued. "This is my request. I can't leave my property untended forever. Lillian, would you take over the running of the boarding house? When the coast is clear, maybe I will come back to join you."

"What?" Lillian's spoon dropped to the floor.

"Live here. Find boarders. Provide meals. You will keep most of the profits which, I assure you, outdistance a teacher's meager pay. And you can be far freer to express your own ideas and live life the way you wish."

"But my mother, my little brother..."

"They are welcome to a room here, too." Emma was in full promotion gear, hoping for agreement.

"Why...well...such an opportunity..."

"Take your time. You have until morning to consider."

"I...goodness!"

"While Lillian dithers, would you, Timothy, keep an eye on the property, making sure it stays in repair and the boarders under control? We could even move a bed into the cellar if you would like to move here. There is room for you, I am sure."

Lillian recovered before Timothy did. "Darling Emma! What a joy for a spinster like me to live in lovely surrounds like these." The slight creases at the corners of her eyes settled into laugh lines of delight. She circled the table to hug her friend again.

"It would be an honor to continue in your employ, Miss Prescott." Timothy did not hug her but he did tip an imaginary tipster, having removed his actual hat before the meal which revealed his bald pate.

"Fine then. You both reassure me. I am so grateful. We will work out all the details of payment to you tomorrow, do my packing, and then I will be on my way." She opened a lacy hanky and handed a nugget to Lillian. "This will help you now, to stock and start the boarding house again."

Lillian stared in amazement. She looked up at Emma then back down at the small golden morsel in her hand. "I am chagrined that my good fortune comes at the expense of your own."

Emma replied, "You are right. This hasn't been an easy new year for the Prescotts. But I am so grateful that you are here for us...me...now." She then presented a flake of gold to Timothy. "An opening salary for your service as our caretaker."

Timothy looked at the gold in his rough hand, then met her eyes. Lillian had known about the gold, but Timothy had not. "I begin to understand why Goodwyn Lewis has such extraordinary interest in the Prescott family."

CHAPTER FIVE

SS *Clallam*, Pier One, Seattle
January 8, 1904

The following day was a whirlwind indoors, although the house looked calm from the out. "Can't give Cutter any hints," Timothy said, and he put his foot down with Emma. She was not to leave the house. Any last minute needs would be handled by Timothy or maybe Lillian, if the need was of a womanly nature.

Emma and Lillian vacated the rooms of the personal items from Gran, Ma and Emma. All was carefully wrapped and hauled to the attic with Timothy's help.

"You finish making the rooms ready for new boarders when I'm gone," Emma said to Lillian. "New linens, curtains and such. I couldn't bear to do it or to watch it done."

"Of course."

"I won't take much with me other than medical tinctures and solutions. That's what I most need to start a business wherever I land." Emma also packed a truck to be sent when she had an address. She wrote a Letter of Agreement between Lillian and herself. "I will send money by letter monthly until the house is up and running."

At day's end, they practiced her disguise for the next day. Her hair was pinned under a boy's gray cap. Lillian provided a pair of dungarees owned by her brother Alfred.

"Won't he miss them?" Emma asked.

"Maybe. But he'll never think I diverted them to you. Besides, he's truly outgrown them, and my mother would have given them to the rag man soon enough."

His slicker was overlarge as well since its original owner had been Lillian's and Alfred's father. "At least you need not bind your breasts," Lillian proclaimed. "This coat hides a lady's charms."

Minerva Prescott had used powdered milk of magnesia to pat on her face with a puff. To that, Emma added a touch of boot black and ash, with a dab of boar grease. The resulting goo, spread onto her pale countenance, darkened her skin tone. Standing back to observe their creation, Lillian observed, "You do not look like Emma Prescott if not observed too closely. You could pass for a boy, maybe before his beard begins to show. Stay away from others if you can. Act really shy. Try not to squint without your spectacles."

Fortunately, Emma had heavy boots of her own, used for tramping forest trails looking for wild plants. She lengthened her stride to create a different walk than the one Cutter might recognize.

Emma left for the pier at dawn as the wintery day allowed a cold sun to lighten the overcast sky. She crept out the back door and traveled alone along a dark alley to the street, clutching a boy's scarf around her neck. Allen and Timothy were both probably recognizable by Cutter, so Emma went alone. She felt isolated, naked to danger, and angry to be forced from her home. But, and she had to admit it, she was stimulated by the adventure, as well. Who knew that creeping about in disguise could be rather thrilling?

The only thing she carried was her new doctor bag filled with her eclectic supplies plus a change of clothes so she could emerge as female again when the vessel arrived in Victoria later that afternoon. She'd also placed her blue-rimmed glasses in the bag since they might help a sharp-eyed man like Cutter to identify her. She could see distance well enough, but hoped to avoid having to read small print or thread a needle for the next few hours.

The ferry would arrive from Tacoma and was scheduled to depart from Seattle at 8:30. She knew the SS *Clallam*, launched just months before, was rumored to be a bad luck ship. Timothy had told her the tale just the day before.

"The little lass who was to crack a bottle of champagne on the bow for good luck? She failed to hit it, so the Clallam was launched unchristened. And there's more."

"Mr. Crogan, you mustn't scare Emma," Lillian advised.

"I want to know, Timothy. Go on."

"Her flag was first hauled up her mainmast upside down. That's known across international waters as a distress signal." He paused for a swig of ale. "The two events give sailors reason to distrust the ship."

Lillian protested again. "Such nonsense."

"Timothy is teasing me, Lillian. He is well aware I countenance no such silly superstition. The ship has been sailing just fine for months now." She took a sip of ale herself.

Now, in the dim light and windy cold on the pier, Emma shivered as she saw the *Clallam* enter the bay from the South. It looked minute in the expanse of gray between where she stood and the Olympic Peninsula looming to the west. She gave thought to Otis Combes on his adventure to that mountainous, untamed land.

"Waitin' for the Hoodoo Ship, are you laddie?" asked an ancient mariner, sidling up to Emma. She felt flustered, forgetting she was a boy, but thought quickly enough to nod instead of speak.

"The Hoodoo Ship," her commentator repeated louder to the boy who must be deaf. "Better name than *Clallam*. She'll prove a faithless whore, mark my words." He shook his silvery head and shuffled away.

A jinxed ship. On the folder that held her ticket, Emma read the vessel's bona fides printed by her proud owners:

- 657-ton, 168-foot wooden-hulled steamship
- Launched April 15, 1903
- Cruising speed of 13 knots
- 44 elegant staterooms
- Six commodious lifeboats as well as 530 life preservers.

The folder said nothing about a jinx or bad luck. Emma, reminding herself she was not superstitious, was nevertheless happy she could read no more of the smaller type about her vessel, now that her glasses nestled in her medical bag.

She turned, looking back at her city. This whole area burned to the ground just fifteen years before. She vaguely remembered her mother's fear of the blaze as she grabbed Gran's and Emma's hands to head uphill from their home. The fire had not reached as high as the Prescott Boarding House, but here at the port, there were still signs of the conflagration. The present city rose tall from its past. A new street level far above the tides had risen over the lower layer. The noises and dust of construction filled the air. Masons and bricklayers created buildings no longer made of wood. Skyscrapers muscled their way above lesser structures. Seattle was rebuilding in a better image for itself.

As she stared upward, deep in her own thoughts, Emma became aware of the odor and bleats of livestock. She looked down to see she was suddenly surrounded by sheep.

"Off to Victoria for a Canucks' mutton stew," said a shepherd, passing her by. "Sorry to surround you, boy. Just push through them if they bother you."

Emma touched her hat brim then moved away from the sheep to gather with other passengers arriving early.

The *Clallam* steamed in, appearing sparkly, sleek, and modern. Emma was near the head of the line to board as soon as incoming passengers and freight unloaded. She saw a man with a bell-sheep helping the shepherd load his flock. But the bell-sheep dug in and refused to board.

"Won't do the job she's trained to do. Crazy old ewe's not gettin' aboard today," the dockworker yelled to the shepherd. "No sheep for Canadian butchers, I'm afraid."

The bell-sheep won't board? Jinxed indeed, Emma thought.

From beneath the brim of her cap, she squinted down the line as passengers arrived to queue behind her. Maybe three dozen. Or more. She looked from face to face, her focus better as the distance from her eyes increased. That husky man in coveralls? The one in the stovepipe hat? No, too big or too tall. As she remembered, Cutter was not a large man. Willowy even, shoulders slightly slouched.

Is he here? Have I escaped his notice?

Emma tried to contain her jitters. But butterflies thrashed and her heart pounded. *Hurry, hurry, get me onboard so I can hide.* She realized she was embracing her new medical bag tightly against her chest in a protective gesture. She quickly lowered it to grasp by its handle in a far more masculine hold. She felt the need to babble.

I am a boy, I am a boy, I am a boy.

* * *

Cutter stretched and scratched a buttock. When it was thoroughly dealt with, he moved on to finger comb his hair.

He saw no reason to hurry. He knew Emma Prescott would be on the SS *Clallam*. Somewhere on the way to Victoria he would confront her, and the gold would be his.

He stopped to have a think, not a common activity for Goodwyn Lewis. He wasn't sure which he wanted more: the gold or the chance to cut that bothersome skirt down to size. He was tired of her. Maybe if she was pretty, it would be fun to play this game of tag, but this girl was exasperating. Someone like her should not get the best of someone like him.

While Timothy and Allen had spent the night on guard at the boarding house, Cutter spent it in bed in his digs across the street. He'd avoided the cheap brandy that was his usual evening companion, wanting to be in peak form for his busy day. But he'd nonetheless dulled his senses with a hearty slug of morphine to kill the pain of a newly inflicted facial wound.

Cutter felt rested and, if not exactly sharp, at least ready for action. A local restaurant provided his breakfast which he chewed carefully on the right side of his mouth. Maybe he'd smash Miss Prescott in the face, in return for the wound landed on him by her mother.

When finished with his meal, he sauntered to the dock in time to board the *Clallam*. He recognized the ferry by the black ball on the shipping line's red flag above the crowd. He next admired her single stack, double masts, the pilothouse built at the top of her superstructure. Early passengers strolled her main public deck even in the rain. The Puget Sound Navigation Company had a near monopoly on the Mosquito Fleet of steamers that scuttled back and forth, a lifeline linking Tacoma, Victoria, and all ports in between.

Cutter joined the end of the queue and squinted to scan the long line in front of him. Then he turned to eye the last minute passengers joining him at the end. Couples, families, singletons, business-types, and day trippers. He did not see Emma among them, but it was no worry to him. She was no doubt on board already, congratulating herself for outsmarting Goodwyn Lewis.

Sorry bit of fluff, he thought. *She'll hand over the gold before the day is out. And her life as well.* The Prescott women had aggravated him too much to escape with a mere theft. The more he considered it, the angrier he got. He was losing what little control he had over his thoughts.

Cutter carefully touched the bruising around the gash on his jaw, and he still tasted blood when he ran his tongue gingerly over the space where two lower molars had been. Minerva Prescott had swung that frigging poker with all the power of a three-bag hitter. He'd carved her like a Christmas goose in his rage after that. The grandmother, too. The young one would die today. Cutter would take his time to locate Emma on the journey to Port Townsend, then make his move on the longer stretch between Port Townsend and Victoria. Thirty-five miles of open sea would give him all the time he'd need.

The vessel opened wide for the loading of freight below. It appeared to be mostly food, barrels of butter to bags of onions. The *Clallam* was fitted with luxury staterooms, but this sailing to Victoria, with one stop in Port Townsend, was only a few-hour voyage. Most passengers would stay in the main saloon, dining room and bar. Cutter strolled around the deck, then entered the saloon. It was a large comfortable lounge the width of the ship. Douglas fir benches had sculpted seats for the comfort of guest backsides, and the bench backs were carved with sea stars and leaping whales. One end of the room had a tiled floor with dining tables plus what appeared to be a well-stocked bar. Cutter headed there to await departure. It was a short ride to Port Townsend, and he saw no reason why one small brandy would do him any harm.

* * *

Emma quickly scanned the saloon before most of the guests came aboard. Her first instinct was to take a seat in a dark corner, away from the windows, where the ship's lamps provided the merest of light. On second thought, she realized that was the first place a man might look for someone in hiding.

When a bickering couple with three youngsters boarded, Emma moved close to them. With no small amount of hand luggage, a pram, and an aromatic picnic basket, the family took a while to locate bench seats acceptable to the children and the mother. The father then left his flock. Emma's eyes followed him toward the bar.

She approached the family, picking up a toy and a baby sweater that had escaped to the floor.

"Ma'am," she said, handing over the escapees.

"Thank you, young man," the mother said, smiling gratefully.

Emma sat on a bench close to this group. She lowered her cap as though she intended to snooze, at least until the sixish-year-old invited her to play with his stuffed monkey, the one she had retrieved. Emma remembered a tale she used to read to her class when she was a teacher. As she quietly told the story to the boy, his little sister joined him. Slowly the girl crept onto the bench, then onto Emma's lap. Soon Emma looked like nothing more than an older brother delighting the littl'ns.

The mother watched with obvious pleasure to have a moment of quiet for herself and the baby. "What is your name, lad?"

Emma was struck dumb by the question, then came up with the only name that floated through her mind. "Ah...it's, ah, Otis, ma'am." This incognito stuff was harder than it appeared. The woman must think her an idiot.

"We are the Gillison family. That is Virginia on your lap. And her brother is Jack."

In time, the vessel lurched, the engine roared, a horn blew, and they were underway. The crowd settled on the wooden benches, now that the rocking made the footing unstable. Moments later, Emma noticed a man stroll through the lounge, seemingly interested in other passengers. He was the right size, as far as she could remember. When he came closer, she saw he had a fresh facial wound, a nasty looking gash to his jaw. It was new enough that stitches had yet to be removed. Emma had a eucalyptus ointment that could soothe such red, swollen skin. She reached toward her medical bag, then stopped. *How lame brained!* No young boy would do such a thing. Instead she raised the stuffed monkey closer to her face and continued with her story as the man passed by, away from her newly-adopted family.

Soon the ship dipped in the swells, pushed by a brisk wind. Rain began to patter on the outside deck. The children giggled at the rolling vessel, but Mother Gillison paled.

"I'll watch them should you need some fresh air," Emma said to the queasy woman. "And I have something you might try to help with motion sickness."

It was Friday, January 8. The weather was turning blustery, winds gusting from the Southwest. The SS *Clallam* was only a few months old, at the height of seaworthiness with a load of one hundred souls, when she left Seattle's Pier One on schedule at 8:30 am.

* * *

Goodwyn Lewis was cold. The wind and the spray from the Sound made him shiver inside his oilskin duster, even though his coat beneath was good thick wool. His boots slipped on the sodden boards of the deck, so he was unsure of his footing.

Cutter hated the ocean. He scowled at the endless gray waves which were too damn much water for a guy raised in the high country. When you looked at the horizon, you should see hills, not swells.

He wiped his dripping nose on the back of his hand and slid toward the port door. Emma Prescott wouldn't be out here. She'd be holed up inside, mollycoddled with hot chocolate, probably clapping like a church bell with the other ladies. She wouldn't be hidden away in a private suite either, not with a second-class ticket. He'd find Miss Four-Eyes in the saloon. He just must have missed her on the first pass.

Grateful for this realization, he clambered inside, shook beaded water off his coat, and cast his eyes across the rows of bench seats. He made a pass through the saloon, giving it a cursory look. Dozens of folks, families mostly. No women on their own. Some men, one snoring loudly. A traveling salesman shuffling cards atop his sample case. A young lad playing with his siblings. Cutter's reconnaissance landed him back at the bar at the far end of the room once again. Maybe another gut-warming glass was called for to kill the freeze and clear his sight.

He sat over a whiskey and brooded. He'd never gotten used to the wet of the Northwest, wouldn't be here at all if it weren't for riding with that crazy bastard, Tracy. Cutter grew up in the Utah high country, outside the dead-end town of Beaver. His pa had taught him many things about how bad a dad could be.

As a boy, Goodwyn couldn't shoot for shit to provide for the family table, but he excelled with a knife. He'd rather get close and throw. Field dressing an elk was more to his liking than simply shooting the damn thing. Even his dad had to admit he had his uses. Like in the pigsty. Goodwyn took to butchery, feeling the body still hot with fear and onrushing death. It was a precise art to slice the throat, drain the body, sever the joints. A gun was never Goodwyn's weapon of choice, not when a knife could be so appealing.

He'd hunted in Utah not far from another squalid shack where a Mormon couple bred children, one after another. Thirteen of them. One of the urchins was Robert Leroy Parker, who left his home at a tender age to become an outlaw. Parker changed his name to Butch Cassidy. He was the hero of all the local children, the one who escaped the hard-struggle life. The way Cutter saw it, a kid could work for nothing and get exactly that...or he could steal like Butch.

Cutter had longed to be part of Cassidy's gang. But Harry Tracy was as close to Cassidy as he ever got, and that was none too close. Cassidy was rumored to be somewhere in Washington now. Maybe retired, maybe dead like Tracy. Probably not on a boat, shivering in wet boots.

Cutter sipped his booze while the ferry lifted and dropped, heading to Port Townsend. *Not far now.* The Prescott woman wouldn't disembark there. He knew she had a ticket for Victoria. And an appointment with him. Time for another drink. He'd find her soon enough. There better be plenty of gold left. That frigging gold was his. She needed punished bad if she was spending it. It shouldn't be that hard to bring her down. Easy prey. And yet, she'd managed pretty well so far.

That could not go on.

* * *

The weather was still fractious, but holding. On board the *Clallam*, a handful of passengers braved the deck to watch the ferry claim a spot at Union Wharf in Port Townsend. Larger sea-going steamers rested at anchor around them. One of the curious passengers was a young boy named Otis, also known as Emma.

On the wharf, Emma saw members of a Salish tribe selling smoked salmon and what she took to be both clams and oysters. She didn't know which tribe this was, since Salish people populated the whole Sound. Some called it the Sea of the Salish. She was curious about the herbal remedies all of them used. She would like to try talking with them, but wanted to do nothing to draw attention to herself.

She stood holding little Virginia's hand as Mother Gillison breathed great gulps of air then marveled, "Your remedy may be working, Otis. I feel much settled. What an amazement you are."

Emma was tickled and could not help showing off. "Asians prefer wormwood, and I can get it at the herbalist in Chinatown. But Western folk have luck with white hellebore as long as we are careful not to brew a poison from it. It contains alkaloids which can be dangerous, but I have learned how to use it." If she didn't stop chattering the woman was bound to wonder how a boy not much older than a guttersnipe could know so much. She was sure as eggs was eggs of that. So all Emma added was, "The vessel is quiet here at the wharf. That helps, too."

She looked at the settlement high on a ridge above the waterfront. In a brochure on the *Clallam*, she'd read how ship captains from the century past built magnificent homes with all the Victorian frills. It might have been pretty, but a grey front covered it at the moment like a heavy wet rug.

"Port Townsend dreamt big," said Mrs. Gillison. "It owns the entrance to Puget Sound. What it didn't count on was railroads passing it by. So it's puny again now. Not so prosperous as it hoped."

The port call was brief. The *Clallam* dropped off mail, took on freight, and a group of passengers load. Emma thought that the way they laughed together they must be friends or family. No family laughter for her, not any more. Of course, Ma was never been much of a gigglemug, but Gran always loved to tell or be told a good tale.

At noon, the ferry weaved its way back through the bigger vessels and sailed the Sound once more, running with a southwest wind. The swells pushed her onward from behind. Emma and the Gillisons returned to the warmth of the saloon. Emma, tired of how the roughness of a boy's trousers rubbed her thighs, looked forward to donning her dress in Victoria. She wanted to apply a soothing balm to her burning skin, in fact, maybe she would find the woman's necessary room to do just...

She yelped as a furious wind smacked the port side from the west as the *Clallam* turned into the Strait of Juan de Fuca. The vessel bucked, plunging downward then up again. Passengers not seated fell like pins as the Clallam bowled them over, knocking them into each other. Emma was first to grab the back of a bench and right herself, then she helped the Gillisons from the floor. Bottles and glassware at the bar and restaurant shattered, and luggage careened across the floor. A box lunch overturned, and chicken legs rolled by, along with apples, and a loaf of bread. The brass hardware corner of a small trunk cracked into Emma's ankle, and she winced with the pain.

"Surround your Ma," she called to little Virginia and Jack over the noise of the storm and people yelping. "Hold on to each other. You'll be fine. This is just the wild part of the ride, like taming a bronco. Hang on tight!" She saw their father careening toward his family, lurching from support pole to pole. She grabbed up her own medical bag, then trapped it between her bench and the wall of the lounge.

Sleet pelted the portside windows, along with snow. Emma felt terror of the gale beating the glass with such power. What if the windows gave? The heavy sea rolled the vessel again, so standing was nearly impossible. But she began to stagger from bench to bench toward a large wooden container with LIFE JACKETS stenciled on the lid.

A ship officer appeared, yelling for calm. Passengers were helping each other off the floor. Two crewmen arrived at the life jacket container along with Emma. When she grabbed a stack of vests, one of them gave her a smile and a "Thanks for the help, lad." They distributed to the passengers as the other crewman pulled out emergency equipment. Rope, buckets, an ax...

"Where are the flares?" He yelled to his co-worker. While Emma distributed jackets to the Gillisons, she heard the answer.

"Flares? What flares?"

* * *

Timothy Crogan and Lillian Stiltner sat in the kitchen of the Prescott Boarding House. Lillian had provided breakfast. Allen was now asleep in the parlor, but Timothy would roust him soon. The Irishman wanted to be on his way to gather up his possessions, return, and create a den for himself in the cellar. He planned to move in immediately, to watch the empty house even before Lillian could move her family in.

Timothy checked his granddad's pocket watch which was clipped to his vest. "She should be aboard ship nearing Port Townsend, Miss Stiltner, well away from Cutter."

"We can hope, Mr. Crogan. But please, call me Lillian. It appears we are to be business partners, even though you seem to be something of a roughneck. May I call you Timothy?"

He liked how her eyes seemed to tease. Knowing eyes. Clever eyes. *How old is this woman? Some older than Miss Prescott, surely. How did they become friends?* He liked how the bracelet length sleeves of her cotton day dress revealed the delicacy of her wrists. His interest in Lillian did not feel as paternal as his feelings for her young friend. Something altogether different.

"Timothy it is," he said. "But I am a tough guy, Lillian, not a roughneck. Roughneck implies I am a union organizer, and I have enough difficulty merely organizing myself."

"Organization is my strong suit, Timothy, so our business is off on the right foot."

"Do you wish to re-open the boarding house soon?" He asked as she cleared dishes from the table.

"I must have a think, but yes. Maybe I will invite some of my suffragette sisters. The Prescotts would like that."

Timothy felt his spine stiffen. Was he to be surrounded by women? The kind who wanted equal rights? Would he be henpecked to death? Maybe caretaker was not such a good job after all. "Miss Prescott is a suffragette?"

"More than that. Goes back to her Gran. She was one of the Mercer girls, oh, I guess forty years ago. They were looking for marriage, true. But Gran knew something else about them."

"Ah. Mystery women."

Lillian laughed. "Well hardly that. But Gran told Emma three of them were suffragettes who had campaigned on the East Coast and were bringing the good word to the west."

"Ah. Mysterious rabble-rousing women."

"Mmm, maybe. They wanted to secure the vote for women, but marriage was still a goal. They didn't demonstrate like the East Coasters. They convinced other women to work from within, quietly convincing husbands, fathers, and brothers to vote for women's rights. And each time the men vote, the goal gets closer to reality. It'll happen one day."

"You believe men will vote for women?"

"Well, some women run into resistance. It's why Emma's husband abandoned her. That was his loss, if you were to ask me."

Timothy wasn't sure that all women should vote. What an idea. But he had to agree that Ronan Byrne was the loser here. Ditch a fine girl like Miss Prescott? He wondered why women scared so many men.

* * *

The passengers huddled in grim, pale-faced groups. Those who had been seasick seemed emptied. They hunched in their life jackets, like seabirds with their heads pulled tight into their bodies. Nobody spoke. Or if they did, their voices were buried beneath the howl of the gale, the creaking of the wooden vessel, the shouts from one crewman to another out on the deck.

It was dark even at midday. Little daylight penetrated the icy rain and fog. All the kerosene lanterns had been doused by the crew, a safety precaution or so Emma believed. She felt the wretched despair of being in a situation where you have no control. All they could do was wait for news, but an hour passed before Captain George Roberts appeared. He used a megaphone to amplify his voice over the raging weather, attempting reassurance.

"Allay your fears, good people. My crew and my officers are trained to handle storms like this. I have plied these waters for three decades and seen many such blows.

Our ship is up to the adventure." He squinted out the starboard windows and pointed. "Look. You will see the Canadian coast has appeared. Be calm and brave. Follow orders. We will overcome."

Emma believed the passengers took a collective breath of relief. But as she squinted through the storm, all she could see were the ghostly shapes of rocky shoals amidst the bounding waves.

One of the passengers attempted to stand. The man with the newly wounded face seemed to be searching for something lost. He wavered and fell, then stayed still as the west wind pushed the ship to tipping point once again. Another hour passed. Little Virginia crawled into Emma's lap and seemed to sleep. But with no forewarning, the crew became more agitated than before. Emma saw fear in their faces as several raced through the saloon. Emma was no sailor, but she felt the ship gulley and yawl to the north. It tipped to the side and did not right itself. The mighty steam engine suddenly went still, and Emma could no longer feel its throb.

Terror.

Desperate to hear what was happening, she caught snippets of conversation screeched from crewmen and passengers more seaworthy than she.

"Broken dead light..."

"...water filling the engine room..."

"...coal from the bunkers fouling the bilge pumps..."

"...set the stay and jib..."

She knew one horrifying thing. The *Clallam* was dead in the water.

CHAPTER SIX

SS *Clallam*
Mid-afternoon, January 8, 1904

Passengers clustered in the saloon, some whimpering under the sound of the storm, others complaining volubly. A young couple clung together in a display of affection that would have been unacceptable in most situations. Emma remembered when her husband held her that way, and a sense of loss washed over her like one of the stormy waves. She was wrapped in a stranger's coat, topped with a borrowed life jacket, on her way to an unknown Victoria address in a foreign country. Her family was dead.

Who would miss me if I were gone?

A gust of wind blew an officer through the port door. He knocked into a support pole, then braced himself against it. His hair was disheveled and peacoat so soaked it dripped on the floor around him. His rugged sailor's face had the pallor of fear as he lifted a megaphone and yelled, "Attention! Attention!"

Emma shushed the crying Virginia. With all the rest of the beleaguered passengers, she bent toward the officer, straining to hear.

"The engine has quit and the Clallam is taking on water. The situation is grim and requires quick response."

After a stunned moment, everyone seemed to speak at once. "Are we sinking...will we drown...can we swim for shore...an outrage!"

The officer continued to yell over the raucous distress of the angry, astonished, horrified crowd. "This gale has turned us and is hitting us broadside. We are as close to the Canadian coast as we can get. The captain has ordered lifeboats. Women and children are to be rowed ashore."

A mutinous clamor erupted. Many men were opposed. "What about us...Row in this storm...I will not stay behind...my children need me."

Some of the women also disagreed. "I will not leave my husband...my babes can't swim...is it truly safer out there than in here?"

"There will be no argument about this. Women and children. Topside. Now!"

Crewmen grabbed at the families to speed them along. Emma noticed that one of them stood, a long gun at his chest, as though on guard. The sight of him frightened her more than the announcement.

Will they shoot the people who rebel?

"Leave your bags, ladies. Men, back away. Fathers, you may carry your children up to the boats."

Emma's mind shut down with the shock of it. All she knew was that the Gillisons must be saved, and Mr. Gillison was not in sight, most likely at the bar looking for a bottle that had not broken.

It was chaos as families were pushed onto the starboard deck into the face of the deafening storm. They were wrangled up a staircase nearly as narrow and vertical as a ladder. An officer shrieked, "Hurry along! These steps lead to the quarterdeck where lifeboats were stored. You must hurry, ladies."

Emma grabbed up little Virginia and took Jack's hand. "You take the baby. I have the children!" she yelled to the frantic mother. Emma shouldered her way forward to stay just behind Mrs. Gillison who carried a very surprised baby into the icy rain. His indignant squawks were even louder than the wail of the wind. Freezing spray from heaving waves washed over them as the boat was hurled up then back down. Salt stung Emma's eyes.

"All three leeside lifeboats will launch," yelled the officer as the line filed along like prisoners. "Women and children first." One panicky man shoved his way past the women. A crewman knocked him back. He toppled to the deck below.

I am not one of the women! The thought of her boy's attire ripped through Emma's head, but getting the children to the lifeboats was the only goal that stuck in her mind. That, and fear of the dripping ladder. Holding to it was treacherous. She had placed her feet on the second narrow stair when she was tackled from behind. A hand grabbed her shoulder, she slipped on the drenched step, and went over backward holding tight to Virginia, but losing Jack's small hand. Unable to use her arms to break her fall, she cracked her head hard on the deck. Through spots of black dancing in her eyes, she saw the furious face of Mr. Gillison now above her, distorted with fear. "These are my children. My duty. Get below, wastrel! Stay out of the way." Emma felt Virginia ripped from her arms and saw Gillison grab Jack around the waist. Then they shoved their way up the ladder.

At the base of the steps, people tripped over her body. She felt a sharp kick to her ribs. Petrified, she cried out for help, but her voice was no match for the crowd, the storm, and the sea. She pulled into a fetal position, trying to protect herself as she gagged on the saltwater sloshing around her.

From above, Emma heard a voice snarl, "Get back. Let me reach him." She felt strong rough hands grab her life jacket at the shoulders and pull her upward. A man held her as she wobbled on her feet like a ragdoll. She saw him through a blur as vertigo took hold. It was the crewman who'd helped her distribute life jackets. He propped her against the bulkhead and yelled in her ear, "Get inside, lad. You will be trampled here." Then he was gone.

Emma huddled against the bulkhead. She vomited from the pain to her torso and the roughness of the sea. Stomach still roiling, she fought to focus her eyes. Her legs nearly collapsed but she inched her way along until she reached the door to the saloon. There, she slipped back inside.

The cavernous room was now cold, dark and nearly empty. A few men were inside, one on his knees praying, another sobbing, and yet another singing a dirge of some kind. None paid attention to her. She fell in the aisle between benches as the ship pitched, but when it rolled back, she was able to stand once more. Her own loud cries roused her as she moved on. Soaked and freezing, she had one focus. *I must find my medical bag.*

Emma staggered to the bench she had shared with the Gillisons. She tumbled again, but this time landed on the seat and reached down to grab Jack's stuffed monkey from the floor.

Silly monkey. Always escaping.

The Gillison picnic basket had spilled.

Cake and beans everywhere. Daddy Gillison will be livid.

The bentwood handle of the basket had caught around an arm of the bench, and her medical bag was lodged between the two. Her joy at its discovery was short-lived. Emma leaned forward to vomit again. Then she rolled to her side on the bench, leaned her head against the bag, cuddled the stuffed toy to her chest, and blacked out.

But a violent heave of the ship soon spilled Emma to the floor again. She sat up, dizzy, uncertain where she was. She yelped in pain as she realized her ribs were on fire and blood was seeping from a deep slice on her arm. Something was wrong with an ankle, too. As her memory came alive, her vision and her brain both cleared.

The children! What about the children?

She heard agonized voices above the storm, picked up her bag, and lurched from bench to bench as she limped outside. Men lined the railing, a mourning chorus that cursed the crew, the weather, their gods. Emma worked her way between them to the railing and faced a scene of unimaginable devastation.

A lifeboat was lowered from above. Emma prayed the Gillisons were aboard it. Just as she could see inside, the wooden boat cracked into the guard rail before her. She leaped back as it tipped crazily, tangled in its own ropes. Women, children and rowing crew spilled from the dangling boat into the sea. Below, Emma could see others already in the water, near a lifeboat overturned by swells. Directly beneath them, a woman lifted a baby into the air. Nobody was close enough to reach for the child. Soon Mrs. Gillison and her baby disappeared beneath the swells completely. Emma shrieked along with the others.

Men stood onboard, watching their families die. Their children and their wives, fiancées, sisters. A third boat launched, and a man leaped from the deck trying to land in it, but it tangled in its own lines and upended. He plunged with the rest into the sea.

Are all souls lost? How many have died? All the children? Virginia and Jack?

There was no one to ease Emma's mind. But she knew the truth of it. Anyone who'd made it into a lifeboat was now a body in the clutches of the Strait of Juan de Fuca.

* * *

Cutter was too much in the altitudes with booze to panic but lucid enough for belligerence. He made a pass at the ladder but was instantly repelled by a crew growing ever more violent.

A big man grabbed him by the collar. "Join these fellows and follow me. Captain's orders." He soon found himself in the hold below, carrying out freight to throw into the sea.

Bundles of bricks and shingles, boxes of farm produce. God knows what all they were discarding to lighten the load. He hated the idea of tossing riches into the hungry sea.

Then he remembered the freight that made him board this hell ship to begin with. Emma Prescott and the gold. Both now lost at the bottom of the sea. His roar of fury was drowned as he hoisted bags of potatoes overboard. How in tarnation had he missed Emma onboard? A pox on all the Prescott women.

He saw male passengers join the crew to bail water. Those below deck filled buckets, then a brigade of desolate men lifted them up a ladder to dump overboard. Their only hope seemed to be removing more water than was coming in. Cutter saw the level rising, and it was enough to sober him. When the freight detail was done, he would bail to save his own skin. The riches of the lost cargo ceased to call to him.

* * *

Emma limped as far astern as she could, fighting the wound to her ankle and the sway of the ship. Through the saloon, dining room, bar, and into a narrow passage between private staterooms. This was not where her ticket would normally take her; a cabin boy would turn her back to the other end. This was for those passengers wealthy enough for private quarters.

Nobody was around to keep her out. The sea didn't care what class a person was from. Dead was dead.

Most cabin doors were open. Emma pushed one wider. "Hello?" she called. "Anyone here?"

No answer.

She entered the tiny cabin which had a built-in bed, dresser, closet, and little else. Even the first class must use the public toilets. "Not so haughty-taughty after all," she jabbered aloud to no one but herself. "Why did I say that? My mind is elsewhere. This must be shock. Have I an herb for that?"

Emma sat on the bed and opened her medical bag. She uncorked a small bottle of morphine syrup that she had purchased at the apothecary and drank from it. Now she'd have nothing for teething babies should the need arise. "Oh well," she babbled on. "A career in medicine? Might as well pull the string on that bathwater." Any future at all seemed very far away.

Slowly, she removed first the life jacket, then the oversized coat and then the boy's shirt, experiencing fierce pain in her ribs as she flexed her arms. There was little she could do about it but wrap her torso and await the morphine's blessing. She pulled a linen sheet from the bed and, with the help of Cutter's knife, shredded it into strips. "That's the one good thing you've done for me, Mr. Lewis." It made her giggle, as did the thought that cutting up the bedding was a very second-class-person thing to do. False laughter turned to very real tears when she stood to create a mummy wrap around her ribs.

She sat again, now stiff from the binding. For her next repair, Emma removed needle and thread from her bag. There was no water in the room to clean herself, only the remains of a pitcher and wash bowl broken by the bucking ship. The morphine was working its magic, or she never could have done what came next. She removed her glasses from their case in her medical bag, placed them on, and stitched the rip in her own arm. It was difficult work in the dim light of the afternoon as her glasses kept gathering the salt in the air and the salt of her tears. When the stitching was done, she replaced the spectacles in her case and buried them in her bag.

As she put the shirt back on, Emma realized her pain had drained away, but her tears rolled on. Exploring her ankle for a possible break, she decided it was sprained but, on the whole, believed it would do with a bit of rest. "I'll lie down for just a moment," she said to invisible listeners. Emma felt secure in this cabin, hidden from Cutter if he was actually onboard. If she were to die now, it would be from water, not from his blade or a gun. She shut her eyes to see if she could rid the sight of Mrs. Gillison reaching up with her baby.

Alas, Virginia and Jack. Her grief was inconsolable.

If waves were to wash over the ship and break it to bits, if water in the hold was to rise up and cover her, Emma truly did not care. Not at this moment. She was drained of hope, drained of will. Pain, exhaustion, and morphine overcame her, and her consciousness was lost.

* * *

They were in the kitchen of the Prescott Boarding House.

"Is it now to be the Stiltner Boarding House?" Timothy asked as he worked.

Lillian, at the kitchen table, looked up from the rental listings in *The Seattle Star*. "Well no, of course not. This will always be Emma's house."

"That's the proper thing, Lillian." Timothy, on his knees and with sleeves rolled, was cleaning the wood burning iron stove. Allen's ballbat was not far away, although they didn't really expect a visit from Goodwyn Lewis. They believed he must have given up on Emma and her gold. If he was watching the house, he would not have seen her. Still, you never knew, and Timothy was a keen practitioner of vigilance. He was a battle-scarred product of his Irish roots and knew how often trouble could break through any door.

Lillian said, "Minerva Prescott was a traditionalist about that old cooker of hers. But I am sure Emma would allow us to consider gas. Or even the new electrical stoves I have heard about. Amazing devices, so they say."

"Wood is plentiful, cleaner than coal, and it gives me something to do. I am content with it if you are," Timothy said.

"You have a smudge on your nose," she said.

"Would you like one as well?"

"I will pass on that." She handed him a soft rag. "I tell you, Timothy, this boarding house idea is a prickly cactus."

"Why is that?"

"Well, the difficulty is whom you allow to call it home."

"Not just those who can pay for it?'

"Apparently not. Mrs. Braxton lets suffragettes work in her home, but they don't live there. She told me if I were a matron only to females, people would suspect I am secretly running a...a...house of ill fame." She ended in a whisper.

Timothy snorted once before controlling his laugh. Clearly, if women with the dress and comportment of Lillian Stiltner thought they would be confused with wagtails, they had rather limited exposure to the concept. Not that he would admit he knew what a real brothel was like. He did not know if Lillian would appreciate his candor or merely find him to be a practitioner of horse's assery. And he wanted to be in her good graces. He tried for solemn consideration of the issue. "I can see that as a potential concern, yes, indeed."

"But! My mother says that it cannot be co-ed lest ladies meet objectionable men. Foreigners and the like."

"Gadzooks. I do hope I am not objectionable as caretaker to your mother's way of thinking."

"I am sure she would prefer a couple of burly women, but you will have to do."

When he saw her smile he realized he was being teased. Like him, this woman could detect the humor in a situation. They chuckled together. Then he suggested, "You could provide board to men only."

"How would I ever keep up with the laundry and control the language?"

"It is a puzzlement, Lillian."

"I believe I will rent to any soul I find acceptable. Single women or families or well-to-do businessmen or poor poets. Would you agree?"

Timothy Crogan was glad they would house more than suffragettes although he was sympathetic to their cause. He knew how he'd fought for Home Rule back in Ireland...and lost. Could wanting to vote be so different from that? But still. Surrounded by them? Maybe not so bad if they were all like Lillian, a woman he was beginning to think of as his Lillian.

"It all sounds good to me. Well, maybe not a poet. He might woo you with his words and expect boarding for free. No, definitely not poets, poor or otherwise."

"I have read the Irish poets, Timothy. You are definitely a ... sensitive people by your words."

"It is more than our words, Lillian. We have feelings, too."

She stared straight into his eyes, and it surprised him because women so rarely did. Her long black lashes, the whites free from the redness of booze and smoke, the clear sky blue. It was breathtaking.

For the love of God, I may swoon.

"It is your sensitivity, Timothy," Lillian said, "that assures me I should go to my own home tonight. You may walk me there, if you wish, before you return here for your first night as caretaker. I will move my mother and brother tomorrow. After that, I will move in myself."

He thought his heart might break at losing her for the evening. However, it was only right. They could hardly stay in the same house with nobody else there. He best get his goggly-eyed head back on the issue of the whereabouts of Goodwyn Lewis.

* * *

When Emma awoke she felt both better and worse. Her vertigo was gone, but her arm, ribs, and ankle were swelling, bruising, and doing the other protective things a body does. Emma knew that sleep had been the best balm of all, or she would not have used the morphine.

As her head cleared, a bolt of fear raced through her. With it came the delirium of a mother and baby, drowning in the raging sea.

Are we sinking? But wait! Emma realized how little she could see. She'd come to this cabin in the afternoon, but now it was pitch as night. She was astounded by how long she'd been unconscious. It must have been hours.

Yet we're still afloat. How can that be?

The only light was a faint glow coming through the porthole in the cabin. Emma slid from the bed onto her feet with a moan, then limped to the porthole.

Are those lights from another boat?

The movements of the *Clallam* seemed different. The steam engine was silent and the ship continued to rock, but less violently now. The wind had lost some of its howl, and the precipitation she heard sounded more like rain than driving sleet. The ship's motion seemed to be a forward jerk as well as back and forth.

Are we under tow? Has a boat rescued us? Relief soothed her spirits, warming her as it rushed through her body.

Hot tea. Biscuits. Emma realized how hungry she was. And how thirsty. She turned back to the bed, tapping its soft surface until she touched her medical bag. She would need both her hands if she were to negotiate in the dark, so she used Cutter's knife to cut more bed linen into strips. When she was finished, she positioned the medical bag on her back over the life jacket and wound bedding strips through the bag handles, tying them around her chest.

As she worked, she became aware she was pushing her hair out of her eyes. It hung damp on her shoulders, strands curling tightly in the salt of the sea. Emma had lost the boy Alfred's cap as well as her hairpins.

"Blast!" she cursed, but it was far too dark to search out her disguise now. She felt her way along the walls to the cabin door. The bag, with everything she owned inside, felt heavy on her back but its weight was somehow comforting. Like she was better grounded and more secure. With one hand brushing along a wall and the other arm held out in front of her to deflect obstacles, Emma crept along the first class passageway.

When she entered the cavern of the saloon, through its many windows she could see lit lanterns swinging on the deck and hear men yelling in excitement. Emma exited to the deck, where the bluster lifted her hair into a wild whirlwind around her head. Men were fighting their way up the ladder to the pilothouse, shoving, yes, but with some sense of order. A few called to a boat in the distance, others laughed in hysteria, one bit his lip in fear until it bled. From what she could piece together, a tugboat was pulling them forward while a second tug stood by.

We are saved.

But then a crewman saw her there on the deck. His mouth gaped. He must have a sailor's stock of superstitions because he finally shrieked out a sound. "Ghost woman! Banshee! Here to take revenge on us men!" He turned and fled, slipping repeatedly on the deck, continuing his cries.

Another man she did not see screamed, "She's pulling apart. Save yourselves. We're going under..."

Emma moved toward the ladder, but there, another man gaped at her. He was the one with the ragged gash on his jaw.

"You," he said, baring his teeth like a rabid dog. "Miserable twat. I found you. First the gold. Then you die like the gibfaces before you."

Emma was staring into the face of madness, the face she knew must be Goodwyn Lewis. An explosive fire of rage sizzled through her fear. She snarled, "Cold-blooded snake," at this wretch who murdered her family.

Cutter grabbed at her. She escaped his clutches but he leapt forward, pushing her hard into the railing around the deck.

"The gold, bitch," he fumed in her ear above the wail of the storm. He seized her hair, spun her around, jammed her into the railing again, and wrenched the medical bag from her back. As the linen strips tore loose, they flayed at her ribs, and she screamed, falling to her knees. The bag popped loose and clattered to the deck. Emma grasped it, beating Cutter to it. With both hands, she swung it around, into the gash already on Cutter's jaw. He fell back, staggered, then came at her with a roar. She slammed against the railing again. Weakened by the pounding it had taken from the lifeboats, it at last gave way. Emma tumbled head first into the roiling sea below, her arms wrapped around her bag.

Her flight ended when she smacked onto the water flat on her front, a great belly flop of a landing. It stung like hell and knocked the air out of her; saltwater flooded her mouth. She may well have sunk if it weren't for the life jacket. It alone kept her boots and oversized clothes from pulling her under. She heard others in the sea, crying out for help, but she saw no one through the dark. Only the low light of a faint watery moon battled its way through the last of the storm. The lights of the tugboat pulling on the carcass of the *Clallam* were far ahead, and the other boat must have moved to the vessel's port side. As she watched the *Clallam* seemed to crack in two, its upper decks sliding from the lower.

Was Cutter out here, too, or still aboard? Maybe she'd killed him. Maybe he was just inches from her in the dark. She had no idea. She must leave the area to get away from that threat. And she needed to get out of the wintery water.

As she bobbed and treaded, holding her bag to her chest and paddling with one hand, she realized through the moon glow refracting in the water that the swells were full of debris. The *Clallam* was in its death throes. Boxes and doors and broken beams surfed back and forth in the waves around her. If one such object hit her, it could knock her into oblivion.

A large piece of carved wood came her way, and she grabbed hold, moving along with it. Her fingers felt an indentation along the long edge, identifying by touch a pattern of starfish and whales. Tugging herself to its end, she felt a sleek wooden curve. It was the arm of a bench like the ones in the saloon. Emma felt for the seat and realized the bench was floating on its back with the seat side up in the air. That meant there would be a curved surface, like a coffin-sized cup, above the waterline, maybe a safe haven. Emma heaved her bag up then herself, pulling on the bench arm with her own arms and inching like a worm until her upper body was cradled by the seat. She was exhausted but managed to drag her legs onto the seat without upsetting the bench.

There in the dark, she shivered in the cold air and terror of the sea around her. She could feel her pulse drum in her head and heard herself whimper like a frightened animal. More than anything, she wanted to curl up where she was. But she couldn't. She had to paddle away from the ship debris that could sink her and from the man who would kill her. Resigned, Emma reached down and unlaced her boots. She removed them, then tied the laces together through the handle of her bag and around the arm of the bench, so neither boots nor bag would be lost. She trembled as she lowered herself back into the water, sliding in as far as her waist. Trying to convince herself a rescue boat would come along soon, Emma began to kick.

She paddled a few yards before she felt the bench jerk and swerve in the water. A large fish hit it, flopped onto it.

A shark? No...another person. Cutter?

"Who are you?" she cried.

The dark form moved closer. In the dimness, she recognized the crewman who picked her up when she fell onboard, the same one who'd helped distribute life jackets.

He moved his face toward hers and said, "You! You're the lad. But no, not a lad!"

She remembered her hair, now wet and wild around her. "I confess to you, sir, I am not."

"But you are paddling the wrong way, Miss. We need to head toward a tugboat if we can."

Emma had little reason to trust a man, much less a stranger. But then her brain filled with an image of Timothy. And she heard her mother proclaim that strangers are often more dependable than husbands. Emma made a fast decision to tell this crewman the truth, or at least part of it. "I must steer clear of the man who wishes me dead. He's the reason I am incognito."

"But, safety is with the boats."

"Your safety, sir, but not mine."

A moment of silence. "But I can't leave you."

"Of course you can. Save yourself but leave me this bench."

"I won't. As a crewman, it is my job to protect you. We will go this direction if you wish. I know a place not far from here. Very few miles if we stay on course."

Emma thought a crewman's loyalty should only go so far, but she was in no position to argue the point. She needed him to stay with her. "Lead the way."

They paddled together. Emma had slept and she was strong, even with the blows to her body. But the mysterious passing time ate at her.

"What happened after the women and children were lost?"

She thought she saw tears in his eyes, but maybe it was a splash from the Strait.

He said, "We were able to raise a sail, and the *Clallam* turned enough so the wind did not hit it broadside. The captain headed back toward the American shore. Crew and passenger men bailed for hours to the point of exhaustion. It kept us going, but we were slowly sinking nonetheless when the tugboats appeared."

Conversation stopped then. Emma fell into a rhythm with her kicking feet, a rhythm that matched the crewman's. Time passed, maybe an hour, probably more. She could not tell as the sea numbed them. Maybe they were going in circles. Or the cold would kill them. At last, she drifted away from the remains of morphine and the very real problem of hypothermia.

Breaking dawn revived her. She realized that the massive swells were now tame waves lapping at the bench. Her feet settled on a sea bottom of sand and pebbles. Emma tried to stand but instantly fell back into the curved seat of her little boat. Her swimming partner was not there.

The bench was lodged in the shallows of a land mass. As she looked up, Emma could make out little more than a lighthouse beam blinking away, but she heard dogs barking in the distance. Maybe their cacophony would awaken the light keeper.

CHAPTER SEVEN

The Stiltner home, Seattle
January 10, 1904

A cartage company moved Lillian's mother and younger brother into the Prescott Boarding House the day before, and Lillian would move today. Her muscles were sore from packing and lifting and her ears from the complaints of her mother. Lillian heated water and made herself a cup of tea to have a quiet moment to herself before her workday began.

She thought about Timothy Crogan. In fact, she'd thought about him more than once in the four days she'd known him. His wide mustache and bald pate gave him a disarmingly charming demeanor, but his facial scar, thick neck, broad chest, and rough hands spoke of a powerful background which raised her attraction to, well..."See here," she scolded herself, shaking her head to dislodge his image. "Such images lead to no good. No good at all. But still..."

Lillian had not read the *Seattle Daily Times* from the night before with its first sketchy report of a shipwreck off the coast. She'd been too tired for the evening paper. Now she heard the morning news slap against the front door. "Rude lad," she muttered regarding the paperboy. She opened the door, picked up the newspaper, then dropped her teacup, and leaned against the doorframe for support. The headline of *The Seattle Post-Intelligencer* screamed:

FIFTY-FOUR DROWN IN
WRECK OF THE CLALLAM

Lillian cried out, then snatched a cape from the coat tree and rushed down the street, newspaper tucked under her arm, all the way to the Prescott Boarding House.

"Timothy!" she gasped, out of breath as she burst through the front door. With an intake of air, she tried again. "TIMOTHY!"

She stood crying, her delicate hands over her eyes, until Timothy appeared, holding a screw driver. He dropped the tool, then put his arms around her.

"What is it? Lillian, my dear. Are you hurt?"

She could only sob against his shoulder.

"I was installing locks on those parlors windows," he said as if she needed an explanation. "But then I heard you."

"I'm okay. It's just..."

He sounded possessed with outrage. "Has someone hurt you? I will pound the living hell..."

"I...I'm not hurt," she said drawing back from him. "But look." She handed over the paper which she still clutched beneath her cape.

He let her go to take the newspaper from her. She watched as the headline that had bludgeoned her did the same to him. Photos, illustrations, even a map reported the wreck of the *Clallam*. Over fifty drowned. All women and children lost.

"All women and children?" he questioned. "All of them?"

Emma, Lillian thought, and she was sure he was thinking the same.

Right then, they both learned a life lesson: grief is love with no place to go. The devotion they both felt for their young friend gave way to intolerable sorrow.

Of the two, it was Lillian to first offer comfort to the other. "Let's think, Tim. It may not include Emma. She was dressed as a boy. Remember? She wore my brother Alfred's toggery. Emma may yet be one of the survivors!"

They went to the parlor and sat together to read the full article.

"Lillian! What are you doing that close to Mr. Crogan...whose arm is around your shoulders?" demanded her mother as she passed by the parlor, peered in, and braked to a stop.

Timothy pulled away.

Lillian snapped. "At the moment, Mother, I am more concerned with the whereabouts of our landlady than the whereabouts of Timothy's arm."

Her mother humphed and with a great rustle of skirts, continued on her way.

Lillian sighed. "I'll have to apologize for that, or there will be no end in sight."

"The fault is mine," Timothy said.

"Yes. But I like your arm right where it was," Lillian answered.

Timothy encircled her shoulders again, and they talked sadly about what to do next. They concluded there was nothing to do but follow stories in all the major newspapers. Otherwise, they must wait to hear from Emma, or about her if the news was bad.

In the meantime, they would move forward with their plans to keep the Prescott Boarding House up and running. But the joy had drained away from the activity. And the whereabouts of Cutter ceased to matter very much to either of them.

* * *

The crewman was alive, tossed on his back like flotsam onto the beach. He was spread eagled next to their life-saving bench in a deep stupor, but Emma had listened to his chest and felt his neck for pulse. "You are alive, as am I," she said to the comatose man. "But I am concerned for your poor arm."

What if he did not recover? She chided herself. "See here, Emma. You are a physician. That is no way to think. Your job is to attend this patient, not throw up your hands in worry." Patting the unconscious crewman's shoulder, she added, "You will be fine, sir. But you should know I blather when I am nervous. Such as now."

As the sun rose exposing the murky morning, Emma made out the form of the lighthouse in addition to the light of its beacon. It was high on a sandy ridge above them. The beach stretched as far as she could observe in both directions. When she could at last see the crewman clearly, she huffed at the condition of his arm.

"That won't do. It won't do at all." She used a low voice, hoping to soothe but not awaken him. It would be best if he were oblivious for a while longer.

His arm below the elbow bent in an impossible direction. Emma sat in the sand beside him and opened her soaking medical bag. "Of course, everything not protected in vials or tins will be laden with saltwater." She removed her glasses from their case in her bag and waved them in the air to throw off extra liquid. "Yes, I am a four-eyes should you choose to laugh, but you are not looking your best at the moment either." She donned her salt-streaked spectacles then reached over to brush his wet blond hair from his closed eyes. "Now then, we begin to set you to rights."

Gently, she cradled his broken arm to move it outward from his body, hoping to stop contraction of the muscles.

Then Emma unbuttoned his sodden peacoat and shirt. Holding his good arm upward, she pulled the coat off it, but the shirt sleeve was too soaked for trouble-free removal. It stuck to his skin. "Ah well," she said. Next, she knelt on his good side and rolled him a quarter turn, removing the coat from around his back before lying him flat again. He whimpered but stayed in his stupor.

Sliding the coat off his broken arm was easy enough. "I have saved your coat, but you will need a shirt when we are done." She removed Cutter's knife from her bag and cut through the linen sleeve all the way to the upper arm.

She peered at the break then smiled. The severed ulna pushed at his skin, but neither end of the bone had broken through. "Good news. Seawater will not have infected it." As she explored with her fingers, she thought the radius must still be intact. "Even better."

Emma sat back on her knees and stared at her patient for a moment. Other than a couple cadavers at school, she had not seen a man's naked chest since she was married to Ronan. This one was more slender, a rangy frame instead of a compact Irishman. It amused her that here on this unknown land, shivering with cold and pain, she could still feel the warmth of physical attraction. Emma had enjoyed sex although she would never have told her mother such a thing. Of course, if Ma was reading her mind just now, that jig was up. She giggled through teeth chattering with cold.

Stop this. Be serious. Get the job done.

Her own rambling thoughts were a clear message to the newly certified eclectic physician that she herself was in no fit condition to last long on this vacant stretch of sand. She must find shelter soon. She required warmth, food, drink, and comfort as much as her patient did.

Emma dug wet gauze from her bag, then searched the beach for a length of driftwood, straight and strong despite its days at sea. She wrapped the branch to the man's arm with the gauze, taking care to align the broken bone. "Okay, here we go, Mr. Crewman." She pulled it tight.

He shrieked himself to responsiveness. "What in the...who?" Then he sank back into a haze.

With no means to create a fire to make a restorative tea from her herbs, Emma settled on the remains of the morphine. She dug it from her bag, positioned herself beside the crewman's head, and slapped his cheek. "Awake, now. Awake!"

He sputtered, made a grab for her hand, then yelped at the movement.

"Drink this," she ordered, cradling his head and holding the morphine vial to his mouth. It brought on a bout of coughing.

"Are you poisoning me, woman?" he gasped.

"My intent is to bring you enough relief to climb the ridge to that lighthouse. I can give you more pain assistance there. Your arm is broken."

"I thought as much. It felt so when I fell from the vessel."

He went the night this way, paddling with his legs although his arm was useless? Never complaining of the ache?

She replaced her hand on his cheek, this time to cup it, not to slap. "I have set the bone. I apologize for the discomfort it caused you."

Emma cut apart the rest of his shirt to fashion a sling, then tied it around his neck. After that, she laced on her soaking boots and reloaded her bag.

"Is that a pack of dogs I hear?" he asked, his forehead cross-hatched in a frown.

"Sea lions down the beach." She could see them now that there was enough daylight.

"Are we here alone?"

"I have seen no other...survivors." She could not get herself to say bodies. "But keepers from the light will surely see us soon. Or someone else on this island if island it be."

The crewman struggled to sit up. As he focused on their surroundings, she worked her fingers through her tangled wet hair. She said, "Tell me your name."

"Severin Eronen. Some call me Sev."

"I'm Emma Prescott. Do you know where we are?"

He smiled. "We stayed on course while we swam. This is Smith Island. Closest land to where we ditched the *Clallam*."

"Or where the *Clallam* ditched us."

He looked at his arm, wrapped and in a sling. "So you did this, Emma?"

Before she could reply, they heard a call from the direction of the lighthouse. A man yelled "Hallooo," and waved his cap at them. Emma waved back. As she watched, the stranger replaced his hat and picked his way down the face of the cliff. Then she gasped.

An enormous bear bounded down the ridge toward them, far faster than the human. No, not a bear. A huge black dog. And yes, this one was a real dog, not a sea lion, with a joyous bark and wagging tail as it tore toward them, sand, grass, and slobber flying.

"I believe help is on its way, my friend Sev."

"We are saved, my friend Emma." He leaned forward and gave her a one-armed hug, then they stood, supporting each other, to greet their welcoming committee.

* * *

Keeper Henrik Bjornman arrived on the beach soon after the Newfoundland dog had covered both survivors with saliva. Bjornman was built like a mallard with a great round chest, and short, scrawny legs. And like a duck, he waddled. Nonetheless, he had donned his double breasted uniform jacket in his official capacity as a representative of the US Lighthouse Board.

"Koira, get away, get away," he commanded the dog as he helped Emma climb the cliff to the lighthouse and buildings above. Her knees trembled and her ribs ached, so his arm around her waist was blissful support. "This dog was the last castaway before you two showed up. Just appeared on the island one day. The Missus named him Koira. Means dog in Finnish. How are you faring, Severin? Bearing up?"

Severin was behind them, grappling up the hill. "I'm fine, Mr. Bjornman. Emma had a liquid that nearly killed me to swallow, but it has minimized the pain in my arm."

By the time they reached the house, Mrs. Bjornman was warming *pulla* bread in the oven and heating an enormous kettle of soup on an ancient iron stove. Emma breathed deep of the rich aromas of cardamom in the bread and mutton in the broth.

"Storms provide us with driftwood when the tender can't get through, but when it can, it delivers us coal," Mr. Bjornman explained. "And call me Henrik. My wife here is Aava, but you'll find she speaks little English. Hard for a Finnish girl to learn the jargon when the only company she has is an old Finnish recluse like me."

Aava smiled shyly, and Emma reached forward to pat her arm. "Thank you, Aava. You have saved us," she said slowly and softly.

Aava might not know the words but appeared to understand the emotion. She touched Emma's hand in reply and said, "Joo."

Soon their clothes were draped around the kitchen to dry. Emma was wrapped in a robe belonging to Aava, and

Severin, tall and lank, wore the pants and shirt of a very short, round keeper.

After Emma rewrapped Severin's arm in dry bandages provided by Aava, the four of them ate. Koira placed his large rump on Emma's stockinged feet while her boots dried near the stove, warming her from the toes up as soup worked its magic from her lips down. She sipped the black cottonwood twig tea she had made from the damp supplies in her medical bag. It would fight inflammation and pain for both Sev and herself.

"I would happily offer you a cup," she said to the Bjornmans, "but it tastes quite ghastly."

"Indeed it does," Severin said, frown lines appearing on his forehead.

"I can help you there, lad," said Henrik as he poured a measure of brandy into each cup of tea. "No alcohol allowed at the lighthouse." He winked then became serious. "Now tell us what you know. We saw lights in the distance, then nothing more. What has happened?"

Severin began to relate the shipwreck of the *Clallam* as Henrik translated quietly to Aava. Emma had many questions, but for now, she chose to listen carefully, collecting pieces of the story that she didn't know.

"The storm was severe, but we could have weathered it," Sev began. "The whole crew has seen worse before. The vessel fought her way across thirty-five miles of open water to within sight of Victoria Harbor. No more than three miles away.

"The gale and the heavy seas didn't stop us. It was the flooding of the engine room. A broken deadlight on the starboard side ushered the water in. We tried plugging that porthole with blankets and nailing boards across it. But water continued to rush in. I don't know from where. The coal bunkers flooded and coal fouled the pumps. Then the fire went out.

"Some of us manned hand pumps, others tried setting the stay and jib so the ship might turn back. Captain ordered the rest of us to load the starboard lifeboats."

Severin's voice quavered, so Emma contributed what she knew. The image of Mother Gillison and her baby flooded her eyesight with tears as she described the loss of the rowing crews, women, and children. "After that, I went to a cabin and nursed my wounds. Then I fell oblivious, apparently for some hours."

Severin finished as much of the story as he could. "During that time, the *Clallam* turned back toward Port Townsend. We were sinking so male passengers still on board joined crew in bailing and removing as much weight as we could. All freight went overboard. We were desperate to ride higher in the water."

"But if you could turn back, why did the Captain order the women and children off the ship?" Henrik asked as Aava discreetly removed the brandy bottle from his reach.

Severin could only shrug. "I must believe he thought it was the right thing to do, when we were so close to shore. A lot of people will be asking that exact question."

Emma was one of those people. But for now, her only question was, "What happened next?"

"The bailing went on for hours until we were all exhausted. Finally we saw lights of a tug coming toward us. It got a line on us and began to tow us to port. We rejoiced, God help us. But the *Clallam* proved too weakened. Her frame began to pull apart. We were sinking fast with no way of letting the tug know what was happening. Men began leaping overboard. A second tug showed. This was maybe five miles from here, maybe less. I can only hope that a rescue boat scooped up survivors. If not, dozens of souls perished."

Four humans mourned the stunning passing of so many others. With little left to say, Henrik showed Severin where he could bed down in a small barn, in the loft above a pen of four fine sheep. Aava led Emma to a back room in the tiny house. Both shipwreck survivors needed rest. Koira, who had decided that he owned Emma, circled his enormous self on the rag rug beside her bed and took up guard duty.

CHAPTER EIGHT

Smith Island, Strait of Juan de Fuca
January 10, 1904

By morning, Severin was anxious to get off the island. "I must report to work, you see," he said to Henrik. "Let them know I am alive."

Emma was eager to tell Timothy and Lillian that she was alive, so she needed a telegraph. But she was not eager to return too soon to Port Townsend, in case Cutter was alive and there.

While she felt Severin's head for fever and checked that the wrapping of the limb had made it through the night, Henrik answered the crewman's comment. "Will be at least three days, lad. That's when the tender boat comes with supplies from Port Townsend. They can take you back."

"Do you not have a station boat?" Severin asked.

"We do. But she's not up to a crossing like that unless it's an emergency. You can't row anyway, what with that arm like that. I hear lighthouses are experimenting with wireless messages back east in a place called Nantucket. But not here. All in all, I'm thinking our hospitality outranks your need to tell the Puget Sound Navigation Company that they haven't managed to kill you yet."

So that was that. Three days with no news, no communication. At least they were safe. Emma told Severin when he arrived in Port Townsend he must seek a bone setter, in case the broken arm needed to be encased in plaster.

"Your doctoring is enough for me," he answered. The words sounded kind but the tone was dour. Pain was never much good on human moods. Nor was a memory of people who you could not save dying in the sea. Emma knew Severin was grieving as much as she.

Their coats dried to dampness overnight. The wind mellowed and rain stopped. Emma decided to explore the island and stretch her ribs and ankle, removing as much of her own ache as she could.

Smith Island Light and its outbuildings stood maybe a hundred feet from the edge of the cliff. Henrik told them the cliff was crumbling, that its rim grew closer to the building foundations every year. Erosion was not a concept Emma understood in full, but she accepted that the light's years were numbered if it wasn't moved further inland from the sea.

The cliff top was pancake flat, covered with a rolling sea of beach grasses. She stood on the brink but saw nothing below except a small boathouse and the sea lions. Koira barked at them from above. They ignored him.

Looking inland, she spied a clump of scraggly trees, and to the north a narrow spit of sand led to a far beacon. Henrik maintained it as well as the lighthouse when the tides were low and he could get to it. "They scare me, those tides. Spent a wretched night out there on the beacon one time."

She saw no botanicals that interested her, although the nettles under the clump of trees would be good to harvest at a gentler time of year. She sat for a while on the stump of a tree that had likely been fodder for the Bjornmans' fire.

Emma was out of earshot from the others, alone in this wild place, now safe from terror of the sea. But the sounds and images of the last day would not die. People tumbling on the decks. Terrible cries. Intensifying the pain of Cutter's wound with the swing of her medical bag. The horror of a mother with no one to save her baby.

Emma's breath deepened until she was gulping. She slipped off the stump and onto the ground as great sobs erupted from her chest. *Little Virginia and young Jack. Gone with the rest.*

Koira sat, leaning against her. Emma had never owned a dog; she had no idea how much comfort they carried within their hearts. She pressed her face into his neck and cried loud and long.

Why am I alive when so many died?

Why was I the one in boy's clothing?

What more should I have done?

Koira had no understanding of survivor guilt. But the Newfoundland was built for rescuing shipwrecked souls. He allowed this castaway to spill the ills of her world onto his muscular neck. It was a job he was born for. In time, his stalwart devotion drew her from her misery. She sat up, rubbed yet another bath of salty tears from her eyes, and stared at the big black dog whose impossibly long tongue dribbled on her arm.

"Do you have a lady you miss?" she asked him. "Did you fall from her boat and her life?"

Koira kept his secrets. Emma and her dog stood, one of them squaring her shoulders while the other dashed away to annoy cormorants trying to land. When she returned from her walk, Emma was in control once more. She found Severin in the tiny sitting room.

"Ah! I was about to come find you," he said, looking up from the book he held in one hand, resting it on the arm of a sofa.

"Instead I have found you. What are you reading?" She felt his forehead again while she spoke. No heat of fever.

He laughed. "*Robinson Crusoe*, actually. I am learning how to be stranded on an island."

She sat in an upright chair nearest to the sofa. "Perhaps *Treasure Island* should be next."

"I'll check for it in the Reading Chest."

"Reading Chest?"

He indicated a wooden box with brass fittings, opened and upright on an occasional table. "These miniature libraries circulate to all the lighthouses."

Emma could see many books shelved inside, tight against each other. Reading their titles was easier if she squinted a bit through her glasses.

Severin added, "Maybe fifty books at a time, passed on by the lighthouse tender boats. Help keepers and their families stay sane."

"A splendid idea. I shall see if they have *Sense and Sensibility* since I could use more of both."

"Emma," he said and she heard the change in his voice. Levity had left the conversation. "Tell me about the man you are escaping."

Just like that, the nagging worry of being stalked raised its head once more. She'd forgotten mentioning it to Severin but now remembered their earliest words while paddling in the icy water together, a time it was easy to reveal secrets to strangers. She said, "His name is Goodwyn Lewis. Nicknamed Cutter for his abilities with a knife. The best a generous person could say for him is that he is a thief."

Severin set aside *Robinson Crusoe*. "That is not an altogether positive attribute."

"No, but better than the worst. He is a murderer of my mother and grandmother among many others. Now he is planning to add me to his list of kills." She shrugged. "Or possibly, I have now added him to the list of mine."

"I hope there are not many on your list."

"I don't know what may have been his fate." Emma told Severin the entire story, beginning with the break-in at the Prescott Boarding House by Cutter and Harry Tracy.

Severin listened intently, appearing fascinated. Aava walked through the room smiling once or twice, but she wouldn't understand a word so they paid her no mind.

Feeling empty, Emma rose to get to work. She made the mid-day meal for the foursome, did laundry for Aava, created another sling for Severin from a cotton rag, and mended the pieces of his shirt back together. While she worked, Severin helped Henrik clean the glass of the lighthouse Fresnel lens.

In the late afternoon, Koira and his two new friends walked the island together. Emma laughed at her patch job on Severin's shirt and said, "Looks a bit like Frankenstein's monster as described in the book, but maybe better than Henrik's hand-me-down."

"It does the job," Severin responded. "Aava must love having a woman's help. But I can't say a one-armed glass cleaner is any great assistance to Henrik. He'll be glad to be rid of me."

"I can't imagine anyone would be glad to be rid of you, Sev."

Did I just say that? Am I blushing?

"Oh, I don't know, Emma. I have been named the rapscallion of my family."

"Really? Your wife must be terribly worried for news of you. As, I presume, my friends are for me."

"As well as your husband?"

For the second time in a week, Emma told a man the story of her divorce.

"So you have no husband, and I have no wife, Emma. Although my parents plan to put an end to that very soon."

No wife!

"Whatever do you mean?" she asked.

"There is a girl in Finland that is promised matrimony."

"Ah."

"Ah, indeed. I am a second generation Finn here in the New World. My father came to Canada to log Vancouver Island and never went back. Had a bride shipped to him from the old country. Both my parents are determined I will follow their path. The girl may be on her way as we speak. But I don't agree that the customs of Finland should apply to someone who has never seen Finland."

Emma had an opinion on such twaddle as arranged marriage, but she kept it to herself. Her own track record did not make her a matrimonial expert. She merely said, "It's a puzzle, sure as eggs is eggs."

"A puzzle I must solve soon. As I said, my family is very determined regarding my future."

Emma sighed. "As I no longer have family, I feel the lack of guidance while you feel too much of it."

"Here I am complaining while you have seen an excess of death as of late."

"As have you, Sev." It was difficult for the two of them to maintain light chatter without succumbing to the specter of the day just past. It overshadowed everything.

His voice cracked. "I should have saved them, Emma. It's what a crewman does."

Koira barked at them to quit lollygagging and come along. As they continued to walk, now in silence, Severin took her hand. It seemed fragile to Emma, this tenuous bond between strangers who shared the intimacy of survival. She didn't quite know what to do about his hand around hers, but she didn't pull away.

The following day passed slowly. Emma had time to consider what she wanted and what was right and what was neither or both. That night was their last on the island before the tender boat came. She quietly left the house after the keeper was on duty on his light, and his wife was asleep. She opened the barn door with a soft squeak of hinges; the four sheep baaed but soon circled and bedded down again.

Emma climbed the ladder to the loft. When she was halfway up, Severin reached down to help her. Then he held her close with that one good, strong arm.

She leaned into him. "You are a promised man, and I am a castaway twice over, by my husband and by a ship. This is not a beginning with promise."

He rested his chin on the top of her head. "Past or future shouldn't dictate our present."

"I would not have agreed just days ago. But now? I see how precarious time actually is."

Emma knew nothing of Sev. Not really. She would likely never see him again once they arrived in Port Townsend. But to be held like this, encircled, and revered? She desperately needed that. So when he lifted her face to kiss her, she was more than ready.

* * *

In the morning, newspapers from Portland to Victoria began publishing lists of crew and passengers, as survivors appeared or bodies were found on the American and Canadian coasts. The name Emma Prescott didn't surface.

"It wouldn't though," Lillian said with hope, trying to stay positive and tamp down fear for them both. "It was not written."

"True enough, Lillian. We won't give up on our Emma," Timothy said.

Lillian's mother, Edwina, had unexpectedly taken a shine to Timothy. She scurried to refill his coffee cup when it looked near to empty.

"Dear lady! How kind you are." Timothy was not above a spot of charm if it helped win the older woman's heart.

Lillian nearly snorted. Lucky for him the West Coast was more receptive to Irish blarney than the East Coast. Not that the Irish had an easy road of it most anywhere they traveled.

Timothy said, "I went to the Puget Sound Navigation ticket office last evening, only to be told no more information was to be had at the moment. But we must remember, passenger lists are notoriously incorrect. People both departed and boarded in Port Townsend, so the original count was off. And I was told that children's names aren't recorded at all. So no total of the dead can be trusted."

Lillian cocked her head toward her fourteen-year-old brother, Andrew, and said, "Little pitchers –"

"–have big ears. Yeah, I know. People die. I'm not a babe, you know. I can take it." Alfred was wrathy of late to be viewed as an innocent. He wanted to be treated like an adult, and Lillian far preferred he stay a child. She hated his new sullen attitude and the mustache hairs sprouting on his upper lip. And when had he gotten taller than she?

Timothy said, "I have not seen the name Goodwyn Lewis either. Where do you suppose he has gone?"

Lillian answered, "My guess? Back to prison. Or to the Hole in the Wall to find another gang of thieves. Surely our Emma has outfoxed him."

An enormous tabby leapt onto Timothy's lap causing the Irishman to sneeze. To himself, he muttered, "Bloody hell." Aloud he said gently, "Mrs. Stiltner, dear lady, Muffin is loose again. May I place him out-of-doors?"

Lillian grinned. Timothy hated her mother's cat. But the cat loved Timothy. *That's what he gets for all that charm.* She stood and cleared plates. "We must hurry now so I can straighten the kitchen. A potential boarder comes soon. One who claims impeccable references. Prescott Boarding House will be back in business."

CHAPTER NINE

Smith Island, Strait of Juan de Fuca
January 13, 1904

They were watching the horizon when the US Lighthouse Service tender steamed into sight. As the ship neared, Henrik, who had the only binoculars, announced, "You see her flag yet? Triangular white with a blue lighthouse? That's the flag of all the tenders."

The double-masted steamer was bigger than Emma anticipated.

"Near one eighty feet," Henrik said. "Services a lot of the lighthouses on the Strait, so she's mighty seaworthy to do her job." His uniform had been brushed and the double row of buttons polished.

"How does it land with no dock?" Emma asked.

"Doesn't. Crew rows to us with supplies and our mail. We're especially low on fresh water this trip." Knowing the ship was scheduled, all of them had bathed the night before in rainwater captured in barrels and heated in cauldrons on the kitchen stove.

"So they'll row us back to board?" A rowboat was so little, and the Strait was so big.

"Yes...although I'd hold female nattering to a minimum, was I you."

In the crinkles of his face, Emma detected his humor. She sassed him back. "I see why you chose a woman who speaks no English, my good sir. However, I remain befuddled why she chose you."

The lighthouse keeper belly-laughed. "Ah, lad," he said to Severin. "You may be outmatched by this lady you've chosen for a mate. A saucebox, this one."

So their night in the loft had been noticed by the keeper. Both Severin and Emma blushed as they cast a quick glance at each other.

"No worries. Your story stays secret with us." Henrik grabbed Aava around the shoulders and gave her a crushing hug to his side.

The lady you've chosen, Emma thought while the tender anchored as close to the island as it dared. Had that happened? Had Severin chosen her? Not really. Shared anguish brought them together. Besides, she had to admit she'd done most of the choosing. He would move on and so would she once they reached Port Townsend.

The shore crew delivered weeks of newspapers to update the keeper and his wife on progress with the Panama Canal, the Ottawa Silver Seven's win of the Stanley Cup, what that vigorous youngster Teddy Roosevelt was up to in the White House, and the shipwreck of the *Clallam*. The lighthouse tender would not wait for long conversations so goodbyes among the four were quick. Nonetheless, Emma managed to hug her hostess and slip one of her few remaining golden nuggets into Aava's pocket.

Emma had no luggage other than her medical bag as she took a seat in the rowboat. At least that was true until Koira splashed through the shallows and leaped in with her, causing the boat to rock side to side in the smooth water.

"He is your dog, ma'am?" a crewman asked.

"Appears he is now," called Henrik from the beach. "He chooses to continue his journey with you, Emma. You are castaways who found each other."

Emma might have instructed the dog to leave, but just then, she relished his comfort. She managed to contain her 'female nattering' as the boat steadied and was rowed to the waiting tender. She was determined to hide her fear but had very little desire to be on saltwater ever again, even though the Strait had switched to a docile persona. Koira rested his great chin on her knees.

Severin appeared thrilled to be at sea again. "You see how nice it can be, Emma?" he called to her from the bench he occupied. "Just look at it!"

"Yes. Nice." She hoped her smile was less pasty than it felt.

She remained ill-at-ease through the transfer from the rowboat to the lighthouse tender. At least it was much bigger. To the tender crew, curious about their experience, Severin told his story, but Emma stayed quiet, hungrily reading the accounts of the *Clallam* shipwreck in the newspapers she found onboard. The *Victoria Daily Colonist* and *The Seattle Post-Intelligencer* clarified events that she either had not understood or realized at the time.

The tugboats *Richard Holyoke* and *Sea Lion* rescued thirty-six survivors; the estimated death toll was fifty-six, but the papers were not yet ready to call that official. In the days since January 8, bodies wrapped in life jackets were appearing along the Canadian and American coasts as well as the San Juan Islands.

The dead included paupers, the well-to-do, members of a theatre troupe, a Victoria woman with the shadiest of reputations. Survivors, all males, began to tell their stories in the lurid ink on newsprint.

"...the man next to me screamed 'My wife is dead - my God, my wife!" then he leapt over the rail into the sea, never to come up..."

"...the howling wind and their dying cries screamed about us, two score brave men powerless to lend a hand..."

"...by far the greater majority were wild with fear. When the ship was sinking, men tore their hair, shrieked and called to the tugs for help..."

"...at no time was there panic onboard. Everyone acted manly, I tell you..."

The rush to blame ship, crew, or captain was immediate. The *Clallam* was ballyhooed as jinxed, a hoodoo ship destined for bad luck after the bell-sheep refused to load. "It should never have sailed that day," letters to the editor screamed in hindsight.

The captain was criticized for insufficient safety equipment since no emergency flares were launched. The only signal of distress was the raising of the Union Jack, upside down.

Emma looked up from the papers and out to sea. She remembered dragging out life jackets with Severin as another crewman searched for flares that were not there. She was momentarily back on board, fighting for the Gillison family, a battle lost as swells closed over the baby. Emma opened her medical bag and touched little Jack's stuffed monkey, a remembrance she had kept inside. A low whimper escaped her throat and was matched by Koira, either in concern for his new mistress or a desire to chew on the stuffed toy.

Emma patted the dog's head, then returned to her reading. The captain's decision to offload the women and children in waters that led to their deaths was hotly debated, and he was considered negligent for not informing the *Richard Holyoke* that the *Clallam* was not merely leaking.

It was actually sinking before the tugboat tried to tow it to Port Townsend. Under the force of that tow, the ferry was pulled apart with the main deck and pilothouse separating from the hull. By then, Emma and Severin were paddling away, holding tight to their bench.

"Investigations have begun, and inquests are scheduled for both Canada and the United States," she read to Severin then looked up at him. "We are likely the last two survivors to be found." He had come to sit beside her as the tender neared Union Wharf in Port Townsend.

"I believe I'll be called to bear witness at the inquest. I must get back to Victoria." He took her hand." Come with me, Emma."

Emma was dumbfounded. She gawked at him, speechless as thoughts peppered her brain like birdshot.

Go with Severin?

Leave my country?

Give up on medicine?

Do I matter so much to him?

Does he matter so much to me?

Is there anything but grief that binds us?

It was too much too soon. She was juggling so much heartache, fear, and uncertainty that adding another disturbance to the mix was impossible. Besides, it didn't really matter what she wanted, not really. She was free, but he was not. She gave him the only answer that she could. "I can't go, Sev. Not yet. Probably never."

His handsome face looked pained but not for long. Determination muscled its way to the fore. He shook his head, not accepting her words. "Our time together has been short, but enough for me to know you, Emma. I want to be with you. Come with me."

"I cannot."

"Then I will come for you, after I have my say at the inquest."

She touched his lips then quickly withdrew her hand. "No, Sev. Don't make promises. You have a commitment to a girl crossing an ocean to marry you."

"It's not my choice."

"But it is your duty if you have been pledged." She sounded like School Teacher Emma, a side of herself she'd never much liked but found useful when asserting authority.

Severin's determination would not be denied. "You don't know what will happen. I don't know. I will write to you, and we'll work it out. Don't run from me. I'm no troublemaker, not like the villain who stalks you now. But I will come for you just as surely as he."

Capitulation was easier than argument. "You're right. Neither of us knows. But you must give me time. My thoughts are too scattered right now. I don't even know where I will be tomorrow." Emma provided him with the only address she had, that of the Prescott Boarding House. "Write to me there, and your letter will eventually find me."

In front of the townsfolk of Port Townsend, they embraced on Union Wharf before they went their separate ways. As he held her, she said, "Sev, don't tell the officials about me. I must remain unaccounted for, a soul who was never aboard." They parted then, he for Canada and she in search of a telegraph office. She felt the loss of him immediately, but fear soon filled the emptiness. Emma needed to be away. She could not remain in easy sight of the wharf for long, because if Cutter was in Port Townsend, that was where he'd likely look first.

She telegraphed Timothy and Lillian that she was alive and well but still in hiding. Next, she and Koira climbed the long wooden staircase from the lower harbor to the upper town, walking to the massive sandstone Custom House that contained the post office. Inside, Koira sitting quietly at her knees, she wrote her friends a letter with far more detail than her telegram. After mailing it, Emma walked down to Water Street passing restaurants and shops. She found a grocery where the storekeeper wrapped a few items in a package for her.

It was mid-afternoon. Emma and her dog sat in the beach grass on the sandy soil, a biting breeze fighting a tug-of-war with the warming sun. She was a safe distance away, looking first to the San Juan Island, across the Strait, then back at the Wharf District. That rough area looked hardened and abused, a relic of the gold rush years, its bars and questionable establishments tarnished and forlorn.

Emma gave Koira the soup bone she had purchased for him. He chewed in slobbery bliss, but she felt far less joyful.

"What shall we do, Koira?"

He did not answer.

"We can't go back to Seattle, not if Cutter is alive. He's demonstrated clearly enough that he will not give up on hunting me down."

Koira wagged his great tail.

"Yes, you are a most fearsome protector. But this man is a threat I must live with, a shadow that crosses me anytime, anywhere. I've even dreamed of him. Why does your night brain wish to scare you so?"

Koira licked bone grease from his enormous front paws. The job was a big one, and it went on and on.

"The boarding house is out of the question. If he saw any sign of me there, he'd hurt Lillian or Timothy as well as me. Besides, it will soon be filled with people again. I can't endanger any of them. We must go elsewhere, at least until we know for a fact that Cutter is no longer an issue."

The thought of new boarders reminded her of Otis Combes, who had moved to Port Angeles just days ago to take over a dental clinic. He was the only human being she knew on the Olympic Peninsula.

"Port Angeles. Another, what, fifty miles still to the west, deeper in the wilderness? I've heard it is a haven for socialists. Do you suppose that such a thing is true?"

Koira looked up and panted a wide smile.

"Maybe Otis could help me make a start in a totally alien place. Thank you, Koira, for the suggestion. You are most helpful."

She closed the grocer's package with string, then stood and brushed sand from her skirt. "Come along. We have a journey ahead." The Newfoundland picked up his bone and followed, both human and dog packing light.

PART TWO

Port Angeles

Courtesy North Olympic History Center

CHAPTER TEN

Port Townsend, Strait of Juan de Fuca
January 13, 1904

Emma had seen natives a few days earlier. They'd been selling shellfish when the *Clallam* landed on Union Wharf. That was just before the vessel sank in the Strait of Juan de Fuca. Maybe the tribe could help her now.

Please be there. Please.

They weren't on the wharf or at any of the open market stands peddling vegetables, rags, and cooking pots. But she spotted a small band far up the waterfront, away from the hubbub. Koira and she trod through shells and pebbles with enough crunching that her arrival would be no surprise.

As she neared, she wondered why the natives were all wearing items of Western dress. Weren't they allowed native clothing? Maybe full-skirted dresses and wool town jackets were easier garb to wear than what? Elk skin? Seal fur? Maybe they only used Western clothing when they were in a town built by white men. Had the town been built by white men?

Emma was smart with book learning, but she'd never come across answers to questions like these. Being so uninformed robbed her of her usual confidence. She felt shy as she approached the strangers. The men squinted then turned from her, but two old women straightened from packing an oilskin bag and watched her draw near.

Smiling broadly, she called a chirky, "Hello!" and held out a hand. Neither woman moved to take it. Their faces were round as moons, wrinkled and darkened by living outdoors, or so Emma imagined. They weren't at all red, either, as she'd heard them called, but more tea with cream. Their steady stares intimidated her.

After an embarrassing length of time, she withdrew her hand. Maybe they didn't speak English. Using broad gestures to herself, Koira, and then to the West, she uttered, "Me and dog. Port Angeles. You take me?"

One of the women startled her by calling out in a language that had no meaning to Emma. It sounded a jumble of hums and chatter in a whole different alphabet. Emma chided herself. *It probably is a whole different alphabet, for goodness sake.*

A third woman stepped forward, and stopped beside the two others. Emma assessed her to be approximately her own age of nineteen, maybe younger. Her rich black braid was sleek, with none of the mousy kinks of Emma's own, and the girl's eyes were so darkly penetrating, that Emma feared her pale hazel peepers must look blind behind her blue steel-rimmed eyewear.

"What do you want of us?" the girl asked in a low voice. It wasn't welcoming, but it wasn't hostile either, just matter-of-fact. The girl's easy English startled Emma. Where on earth would she have learned it? A teacher or preacher?

She tried a smile again. "My name is Emma Prescott. I must go to Port Angeles. Can you lead my dog and me there? I have this for payment." She held out several flakes of her remaining gold, and the girl stepped forward to look into the palm of Emma's hand.

If these natives would take her, hiking the distance along whatever trail they might follow, she would not have to ask for passage among the boatmen on Union Wharf.

That's where Cutter would be if he was still alive and looking for her. With this band, she could simply disappear. The native carefully plucked the gold from her hand. "Wait..." Emma said, fearing the girl would leave with it, having made no commitment at all. But she was wrong. She watched her go to the others, her black braid swinging down the back of her velveteen jacket, her long skirt billowing in the breeze. The girl spoke with the three men and five women. They talked in that unfathomable language, maybe squabbled. She pointed at Emma, then at Koira who was peeing on a bleached-out beach log. They seemed to be arguing about direction, some pointing West while another shook his head. More squabbling. Then the girl handed the gold to one of the men and came back to Emma.

"We are traveling that direction. We will take you. Come with me."

The other men and women moved ahead of them. As they walked down the beach, Koira sniffed the girl, his head at her waist-level. She asked, "Is he a good hunter?"

Emma had to shrug. "I don't know. But he swims well."

"So he is a fisher dog?"

"I don't know that either. But he saves people in the water."

"Why are they in the water if they do not swim?"

Emma, feeling less informed by the minute, was very glad when the natives stopped. But then she realized they were approaching one of several canoes on the beach. This one was round-bottomed with a prow raised into the air, a carved animal head scenting the wind.

Emma blanched at the sight. "Oh, no! I meant, I mean, I thought we would walk." She was not eager to get on the Strait ever again in a ferry driven by steam, much less a dugout log driven by oars.

"You are one who does not swim?"

"Well, no. But I..."

"We paddle. Much faster. Come."

It was a flat statement of how it was going to be. Emma could go along or stay where she was. Staying wasn't an option.

Several people climbed into the canoe, loading bags and crates, then taking their seats. Emma judged the transport to be thirty feet or longer and three feet wide.

"You sit in the middle," urged the girl.

Emma followed the order. She dropped her medical bag and the package from the grocer onto the bottom of the boat. Holding one of the sides, which was about two feet high, she swung herself in, then sat legs akimbo beneath her skirt. Koira followed her in and circled close to her.

The last of the natives shoved the dugout fully into the water, then joined the other rowers on braces that passed as benches supporting the width of the dugout. The young translator sat just behind Emma.

"We will be there in the morning," the girl said. "The trip requires us to camp on a beach overnight."

Don't worry about me, Sev. I'll just be camping on a wilderness beach with a bunch of strangers for the night.

Emma was swept away into smooth waters in the late afternoon sun, seabirds circling as they mewled and cried. She tried to relax. She failed.

Swiftly leaving the settlement behind, the canoe rounded Point Wilson with its lighthouse and high palisades. In well under an hour, it passed the construction at Fort Worden. This military installation was the northwest side of the Triangle of Fire, three forts built to protect Admiralty Way from hostile fleets. Emma had read about the project for several years in the Seattle papers but never thought to see it herself.

Koira's damp fur, so close to Emma's face, stank. He'd dropped his bone more than once on her foot as they glided onward amidst the sound of lapping waves and squabbling birds. The further they traveled, the more astounded Emma became by the majesty of the Olympic Peninsula. She was close to enjoying the ride. Maybe she would always look for danger over her shoulder. Maybe saltwater would always remind her of death. But she was enthralled by the beauty all around her, enough to soothe her nerves. She had never been so close to snow-covered, brooding mountains before, except on the train to Missouri. She judged these to be gorgeous but imposing at the same time. Their mere presence raised the hair on her arms. Hills of Douglas fir, hemlock, and red cedar lifted from the shore toward the peaks. At the beach of the Strait, a great heron lifted ahead of them, flapping and complaining at the interruption. Mysterious plants lined the shore. Emma breathed deep, dreaming of the botanicals and possibilities on which she would build her new career and her new life.

* * *

Neither Emma nor Severin told the press of their rescue, but the lighthouse tender crew spoke with a reporter who nosed around the harbor. The next day, a small news item mentioned a mysterious woman named Emma, last name unknown, who may have been the only female to survive the *Clallam*. No details were confirmed.

Cutter saw it.

Goodwyn Lewis had been slammed, battered, and damn near drowned when the rescue boat plucked him out of the water. Along with the other survivors, he was taken to Seattle, given medical treatment, and sent on his way with a bottle of painkiller.

Now, after several days of recovery, he felt well enough to sit in a restaurant and read the paper. Her first name was enough for Cutter. Like a sea beast rising from the deep, Emma had lived.

"Hell fire!" he roared, storming out past other diners and shoving startled waiters out of his way. Hatred blazed through his body. Gold no longer had meaning to him. Only finding Emma mattered now.

He went to his room to pack for a return to Port Townsend. He was nearly delirious when his door burst open.

* * *

They had received the telegram from Emma the afternoon before, so Timothy and Lillian knew she was alive, and they rejoiced. They could not spread the word of her revival to one and all, although Lillian did tell her mother. Consequently, the new boarder received a particularly celebratory meal that night.

"A stellar game pie, Mrs. Stiltner," said Mr. Kryinsky, the clockmaker who had moved in that morning. As he dabbed his mustache on her fresh linen, he added, "If this is your standard fare, I am in heaven."

"Oh, it's nothing," Lillian's delighted mother cooed. "Just wait until you taste my daughter's blackberry pie. You will enjoy it, too, Timothy. A wonderful baker, this girl of mine. And such a housekeeper."

Lillian frowned at her. Her mother had decided that Timothy would be a fine catch for her over-ripe single daughter and had been practically posting bulletins about Lillian's virtues.

Emma's letter from Port Townsend arrived with the next day's afternoon post. Alfred, whose job it was to collect the mail, dropped it on his sister's desk. The letter on top had no return address, an occurrence so uncommon with the mail that Lillian guessed Emma still didn't have an address or was hiding her whereabouts from Cutter.

"Emma!" Lillian rushed to slit the envelope with the pewter letter opener. She shook open the flimsy stationary and read.

My dearest Lillian and my good friend Timothy,

Please accept my apologies for sending one letter to you both, instead of individual missives. Time is my enemy at the moment. First, I am safe with minor aches and pains.

The letter told them of her fate onboard the *Clallam*, the swim to Smith Island, the kindness of the light keeper and his wife. It also told the story of Cutter, as far as she knew it.

Fearing Goodwyn Lewis is back in Seattle, I am pushing further west. When I have an address I will send it to you. At that time, I request you ship my trunk.

You may or may not receive a letter for me from a gentleman named Severin Eronen. Please send it along with any other correspondence when I provide an address.

I hope you will write. You are my only family, and I miss you dearly. I am eager for news of the boarding house and how you are getting on.

I remain your constant friend,
Emma Prescott

"Timothy!" Lillian called. "A letter from Emma."

While she waited for him, she shuffled through the rest of the mail. Sure enough, there was a letter for Emma from someone named Severin Eronen, in Canada of all places. And because she was a woman with a certain sensitivity toward such things, she announced when Timothy entered the room, "I believe she has met a man!"

* * *

The canoe followed the shore. Emma figured she could make land if they tipped over so she finally relaxed as much as she could, sitting on the bottom of a boat against a wet dog. She watched wildlife along the waterfront, including an enormous elephant seal sunning himself on a rocky beach. "Even portlier than you," she whispered into Koira's ear. Then, with no warning, the shoreline dropped away to the south, and the canoe headed across what looked to her to be a vast expanse. The oarsmen pulled harder as the craft fought deeper water.

To calm herself, Emma needed to chatter. She turned as much as she could and asked the girl behind her, "Where are we now? Why have we left the shore?" She noticed how pale her knuckles were so she loosened her death grip on the sides of the canoe.

"White people call this Discovery Bay, although we Klallam did not know it was lost."

"What's your name?"

"I am called Willa Hathaway."

"Why do you have a white woman's name?"

"Half of us have white men's blood."

"Ohhh." Emma chewed on that for a while. It was not a pretty picture of what happened to the tribes. "Is that why you speak English?"

"Many of us do."

"But the two women I met on the shore?" Emma pointed toward them where they sat. "They don't."

"Yes, they do. They merely chose not to talk to you."

Emma had to laugh at such directness. "I suppose you think it odd that I requested transport to Port Angeles."

"I think much of what white people do is odd. I have learned not to question it." Willa nodded toward Koira and rolled her eyes.

All in all, Emma decided that maybe a little silence would go a long way. She turned back to the front and passed the time removing bits of twig and dried seaweed from the dog's thick fur.

Long after the shoreline rejoined them, left them, and joined them again, Emma saw several people on a beach below cliffs, some digging for clams. Women smoked fish at a campfire and dried clams on sticks while two men carved a dugout. The afternoon light was fading.

"This bay is near the white settlement called Sequim," Willa said. "We will camp with family here for the night." As the canoe beached beside four similar vessels, Emma looked up toward the woods of fir and cedar, seeing a cabin just within the tree line. Children met the canoe, then stopped and stared wide-eyed at Koira. He was of far more interest than Emma. It was not long before the littlest of them was riding the gentle giant beside the water as the others trotted alongside, hanging on to hanks of his long hair.

The heat from a large campfire warmed Emma's bones as the sun dropped away from the chill January night. Before all light was lost, she rolled up her sleeve and unwrapped the wound on her arm in order to clean it.

Watching, Willa left then returned with a warm, moist mass on a piece of dry moss.

"For pain," she said. "We make it from violets. And what you call bleeding heart. Some bear grease in there, too."

Emma was instantly fascinated that Willa knew such an interesting concoction. She applied some of the poultice to her arm, then unlaced a boot and put the rest on her ankle. Either the poultice or the heat felt instantly soothing.

"Can you show me how to make this?" she asked. "I know about plant medicines but would love to learn more from you."

The two talked medicine, spirit healing, white and native physician knowledge. How to use sweetroot for fungal infections, goldenrod's power to relieve gas, larkspur shampoo to kill lice, and how huckleberry tea might improve Emma's vision. Willa was skeptical of Emma's spectacles as a cure for poor sight; Emma was skeptical that tea made from berries would do her vision much good. But they both relished the chatter, opinions, and chance to learn from each other. It was no longer only Emma who was smiling.

In time, an elder gave her smoked fish, a camas bulb that surprised her with its sweetness, and what tasted like cornbread. She helped the women clean pots and utensils, although none of them spoke to her with the exception of Willa. Two of the children eventually approached to play a version of rock-scissors-paper with this four-eyed oddity. She was given a mat of sewn-together cattails on which to sleep along with two blankets, and she silently listened to the music of the tribe's language as members went about settling for the night. Koira, exhausted by all those little people to worry about, wedged himself next to her on the mat. Far worse for the Newfie, he'd buried his bone and had no idea where.

Emma listened to the lapping water, tribal laughter, and wind in the trees. She was outdoors in the cold night, easy prey to wildlife, surrounded by people she didn't know from a culture that was not her own. Nonetheless, she felt more in charge of her own destiny than she had since her mother died. "I feel anticipation instead of dread, Ma," she muttered into the night. "Good night."

Morning broke pale, watery. The rain had returned in the night, dampening everything but Emma's spirits. Her coat, the oversized slicker from Lillian's brother, kept her nearly dry. Koira, however, was soaked as the canoe continued to follow the shore.

The tribe delivered Emma to the beach at the east end of Ediz Hook, the long spit of sand that protects the Port Angeles harbor. It was mid-day in pouring rain and low-lying fog. A dozen canoes huddled together, and weathered tents and lean-tos pockmarked the beach. A handful of natives sat around fires, some weaving baskets of kelp or cedar beneath makeshift canopies, while others appeared drawn deep within themselves. Emma smelled rotgut whiskey and despair in the air.

"Where will you go now?" Emma asked Willa, feeling a sense of loss for her new-found acquaintance. "Or do you live here?"

"No more. It is a sad place. We go to the Elwha west of here. The river is my home most of the year. But we travel often to visit and trade."

"Would you join me plant collecting in the forest this spring? I used to go with my father. We have knowledge we can share, Willa."

"I will come. In the meantime, take this." She handed Emma a small package wrapped in buckskin.

Some of the tribe members smiled at her, and one even raised a hand before they headed back toward the Strait. She was no longer a stranger.

"When you come back," Emma called to Willa, "ask for the new dentist here, and he will tell you where I am."

Willa laughed and yelled back. "Did I not say that white people are odd? I will use my eyes, not my teeth, to find you."

Emma laughed but when she turned toward the town, her expression turned bleak. Her first impression through the veil of rain was of stinking mud. Wooden buildings huddled on piers just above tidal levels, and sewage drained openly into harbor waters.

Is typhus not a concern here?

She saw a cow wandering loose and townspeople, some in denim and some in suits, splashing through a street of muck, from one side to another, unfazed by the mess. Freight wagons churned the sludge in both directions as well as along several piers, the hammering sounds of construction filled the air, proprietors washed store windows and swept sidewalks even in the rain. Port Angeles was, if nothing else, industrious. Behind the small tract of flat land along the waterfront, hills rose toward the mountains beyond. The town was spreading along the water and nudging against those hills. Port Angeles was definitely unrefined, but looked robust and growing.

Still, its rawness startled her. "What in tarnation have I done?" Emma muttered to Koira, not at all impressed with what she saw. "Well, no turning back. First, we eat."

She trod south up a street named Lincoln, then turned a corner onto First. At the first cafe, she ducked inside. Koira watched through the storefront windows as Emma shook rain off her coat, read a menu board and ordered the daily special, along with a bowl of meat and vegetable scraps that she took out to her dog. The proprietor loaned her a *Port Angeles Evening News,* and she looked for places to rent.

After salmon chowder, bread, and tea, Emma left feeling revived and began her house hunt. It proved arduous, but not because landlords feared a single woman might start a brothel. It was hard because of Koira. "There's a livery stable for horses," one landlady said with a distasteful wrinkle of her nose at the soggy giant. "Maybe you could get the beast a stall there."

Emma's fourth attempt was a family home around the corner from Lincoln on Front Street, amid other houses, businesses, and churches. It was definitely not the elegant domains of the Port Townsend bluffs nor as grand as Prescott Boarding House, but it had an immaculate room to let on a short-term basis. Besides, the landlady had a child who instantly loved 'Big Puppy,' and Betty Axton was a mother who couldn't say no to her little girl. Emma and Big Puppy were invited to stay.

The room was perfect. Furniture was old but serviceable, and the curtains and bedding were a cheerful yellow, as if battling the winter rain with indoor sunshine. A back door beside her room led to a large yard with an outhouse in easy reach and a shed which could house Koira at night.

Emma felt exhausted but had one important chore to do. She walked to Western Union which was a small counter housed in a hardware store. There she sent a wireless message to Lillian with her new address and asked her friend to send her trunk and, oh yes, any letters she might have received.

After that, Emma unpacked the few items from her medical bag: a boy's shirt and pants, a meager selection of her own clothes, her eclectic supplies, the pouch with its dwindling supply of gold, and a bedraggled stuffed monkey she set on the top of her chest of drawers as a reminder of the children who were lost.

Finally, filthy from her travels, Emma heated buckets of water on the small wood stove in her new room and carried them to the tub in the bathroom. Her ribs were stiff, her eyes stung from tears and rain, her buttocks and back ached from the hard bottom of the canoe. Emma lowered herself into the water and sighed. After soaking for a lengthy time, she shampooed and washed with soap she had purchased from the grocer in Port Townsend. From now on, she would make her own. When she was done bathing, she washed her dress and unmentionables in the same soapy hot water.

By the time she went back to her room, Koira had mysteriously found his way through the back door, opened her room door, and was asleep in front of the wood stove. Emma recalled the child who fell for Big Puppy. She grinned, then crawled into the narrow bed and was soon snoring softly. Unlike Koira, she didn't twitch a muscle, not even to chase rabbits through her dreams.

CHAPTER ELEVEN

Port Angeles, Strait of Juan de Fuca
January 14, 1904

The next morning, Emma joined the landlady's family for breakfast, the only daily meal included in her rent. Betty Axton's husband was the accountant for a logging company so, of course, he was nicknamed Axe. "With a name like Axton, it was destiny," he said, smiling at Emma.

"I prefer to call him Joseph, but Axe it is to everyone else. Help yourself to porridge and ham, Emma." Betty filled a coffee cup for her. "The butcher here does up a good pig."

The Axton's child, Birdie, appeared to Emma to be seven or eight.

"How is Big Puppy this morning?" Birdie asked.

"Why, I believe Koira slept all cozy and warm, as if he had a wood stove of his very own." Emma gave the girl a wink.

"Oh good! I worried he'd be cold in the shed," Birdie replied with a straight face.

The two were now conspirators with a shared secret.

"Koira means dog in Finnish," Emma said. "He used to live with a lighthouse keeper before he came to live with me."

"A lighthouse?" Birdie lit up herself, in anticipation of a story, at least until a fit of coughing disrupted her excitement.

When it passed, Betty said, "There now, Birdie. Hurry on. School won't wait for you. Emma can tell you more about the dog when you come home."

Emma saw concern in Betty's eyes, but no more was said about Birdie's cough. Sipping her coffee, Emma asked, "Do you know of a new dentist by the name of Otis Combes?"

"No, but Doc Sprague quit the business not long ago. Maybe this gent is taking over. I heard someone was on his way," Axe said. He wore spectacles not unlike her own, so Emma was drawn to him as a particularly fine fellow.

Betty smiled. "You'll find that Port Angeles is so small, everyone knows everyone's business."

"The office is on Front near Laurel. Just a short walk back into town," Axe added.

Birdie left for school, Axe for work, Betty began clearing dishes, and Emma went to her room for her slicker. The buckskin package from Willa was still resting on the Chippendale chest of drawers. Emma had forgotten about it in her fatigue the night before. She opened it now and spread its contents on the chest. An aromatic pile of wild rose hips. Dried goldenrod and lemon balm. Nettle seeds, chicory, and cedar bark. What she thought was licorice fern rhizome, but there were other roots and bulbs she couldn't identify. These were plants harvested in season and dried, supplies she needed to start her business in these wintry months. For the first time in a long time, her eyes prickled with tears of gratitude, not grief.

Emma had dressed in her best and tamed her curly hair into a tight chignon before breakfast that morning. She took Koira out to the shed along with a bowl of water, the pemmican she'd purchased in Port Townsend, and a "Be a good boy. I'll visit the grocer here this afternoon." Next she washed her eyewear, picked up her medical bag, and headed to Laurel Street in search of the new dentist in town. The office was easy to find, tucked between a dry goods store and the grocery that housed the post office. A weathered sign out front announced the presence of Dr. Sprague, but Emma assumed Otis had not yet posted a new board. His proposal seemed a century ago, yet it had only been two weeks. His office could not have been open for more than a week.

As Emma marveled on how two weeks could feel like a lifetime, she went into the small foyer and took a chair while the receptionist demonstrated the use of a toothbrush to a youngster and his mother.

"...and then you spit," the receptionist said, holding out a cup for the boy to do so.

His eyes widened, and he looked at his mother in great alarm.

"He is not allowed to spit," the mother said, wrinkling her nose at the dirty word. "It is a filthy habit practiced by lowlifes who chew tobacco instead of smoking it as God intended. Imagine having spittoons setting about."

"All right, then," the receptionist said. "Don't spit into the cup, George. Expectorate. Like this." She spit into the cup. "It appears much the same, but is actually a hygienic choice for a better grade of person who cherishes a clean mouth."

A satisfied mother and confused child left the office.

"Ah! Another convert from tree twigs and porcupine quills to a real toothbrush," the youthful receptionist exclaimed to Emma, wiping her hands on a towel. "We shall improve Port Angeles a mouth at a time." She was slightly pear-shaped, the center of her mass below her waist. Her soft cuteness was the kind usually reserved for baby dolls, and it appeared to be her nature to smile at strangers. A wide white collar at her bodice held a selection of darning needles with colorful threads hanging down. "Now then," she said, taking a seat at her desk. "What can we do for you today?"

Emma had been thoroughly charmed by the little drama. How had Otis found such a jovial young helper so quickly on this frontier? "I am here to see Otis Combes. My name is Emma Prescott."

At that revelation, the receptionist changed completely. She turned fire red in the face. Her eyes narrowed and released darts. "I know who you are, Emma Prescott."

Emma, startled, said, "But...I...are we acquainted?"

Then the receptionist shed another skin. Her smile, her shoulders, her attitude...everything drooped. Big splotchy tears fell onto her desktop. "You've come to take Otis back from me," she wailed. "I won't give him up. I won't!"

"Oh my! No, not at all! I don't want Otis, I mean, I want to see Otis but..."

An interior door flew open, and Otis Combes stepped into the reception area, holding a deadly-looking dental tool. "Molly! What in heavens...Emma!"

Molly jumped up from the desk. At her full height, she could still tuck herself under his arm. "She...she..."

"Otis, I am so sorry! I merely stopped to tell you I have moved to Port Angeles. You are the only person I know here, but I didn't mean to upset this lady."

"Ah. This lady is my new wife," Otis said. "I fear there has been a grievous misunderstanding."

"Oh, Mrs. Combes. Let me assure you, I am not here to disrupt your marriage. I am thrilled for Otis...and for you. Please, please don't think ill of me."

Otis looked nonplussed by the situation and sought escape. "Ladies, I must get back to my patient. I will be done shortly. Possibly you can sort things out quietly." He scurried back to the safety of the inner sanctum and shut the door.

Molly sat and sniffled. "You are not here to claim Otis? We've only been married a week."

Emma reached across the desk and patted her hand. "No, I promise you, no. I have a fiancé myself and no need of your husband, other than for a bit of business advice." It was a white lie, well, a great thumper of a lie. But this nervous bride needed to hear it.

Molly gulped. She produced a hanky from her sleeve, dried her eyes, and honked like a goose into the dainty cloth. "Oh, Miss Prescott, I feel such a fool. Of course, you would do no such thing, a lady such as yourself."

"And neither would Otis, I assure you. He is a gentleman of the first order. If you are his wife, then it is the way he wants it to be. I am no threat, nothing at all but a friend."

"I know he asked you, you see. And you turned him down."

Now Emma was startled. "He told you that?" Otis must be less bright than he looked.

"Well, not exactly. I was his tailor's assistant, and I overheard him tell the tailor. So I applied for the opening." A basket of thread sat on her desk, and Molly removed the darning needles from her collar, putting each with its proper color.

"How very lucky for Otis."

"I crave adventure, you see, just like he does. To start over in a new place. I wanted to come West to be a tailor with my own clientele, and it would not have happened for years in Seattle. If ever."

From what little Emma had seen of Port Angeles, she thought it might be even harder to be a tailor here. Local men were not exactly fop-doodles in their fashion.

Molly said, "I know I was not his first choice."

"Oh, well you are now. He has the exact woman who is right for him, doesn't he? How he must love having a courageous partner, where I have none of your confidence and grit."

Liar, liar!

When Molly smiled it was as though the sun rose in the little office. "Oh! I believe I am going to like you, Emma Prescott."

"I already like you, Molly Combes."

They bonded as quickly as magnets. Emma stayed for lunch. Otis and Molly lived above the dental suite. Crates, yet to be unpacked, lined the walls of the room. But the utilitarian space had already been fancified with striped material and flounces at both windows. *Tailor, indeed,* Emma thought.

"Once we urge the dental business into financial prosperity," Molly said, "then I will open my tailor shop. In the meantime, I save us the cost of a receptionist."

"I will need office space as well. I am an eclectic physician, having studied the art for two years. Almost."

While they chattered, Molly heated bean soup, and Emma sliced bread and cheese. All was ready when Otis closed the office below and came up for his mid-day meal.

"Now, then, Emma, tell us your news," he said, taking a chair. "What goes on at the Prescott Boarding House?"

Emma's news left the couple with mouths agape like two startled trout. Emma told them a shortened version of her *Clallam* adventure and her new management team at Prescott.

"And the man called Cutter?" Otis touched his ear where a lobe was missing. "Does he still stalk you? Where is he now?"

"I presume he resides many fathoms under the Strait of Juan de Fuca."

"Thank God for that, Emma. He was a bully who would not be stopped." Otis shrugged his shoulders. "Still, keep an eye out. I mean, just in case."

Thanks for that, Emma thought. *Not like I don't worry enough as it is.* Emma tried to whistle past the graveyard, to remove the fear of Cutter from her head. But she could never quite be sure. She watched for him from the corner of her eye, and often thought she saw him. Wasn't that the tail of his coat disappearing into that tavern? The scar on that face, there in the crowd on the dock...wasn't that him? And would the bastard ever quit treading through her dreams?

Molly, possibly sensing Emma's discomfort, changed the subject. "Now tell us about your fiancé. How quickly a romance has come about for you as one did for me."

Fiancé? Oh God, yes. My prevarication. Emma blushed. "Ah well, no, not quickly. My mother disapproved so I kept it quiet." She wondered when the lightning for this whopper would strike her. "Now, it can be public. And as he, ah, is divorced as am I, we need feel no shame at a union." Emma described a Severin-ish type hero, one who piloted his own boat. A captain of high standing on the high seas. When it came to lies, her theory was you may as well be hanged for a sheep as a lamb.

Molly appeared thrilled. "Perhaps he'll steam into the harbor one day and like a pirate, carry you away."

"Perhaps." Emma thought Molly might have read too many dime novels.

Otis said nothing, but his narrowed eyes told Emma he was not buying her story. "Well, it's been a delight, ladies. Now back to work."

Before Emma left, she commissioned Molly to make her a new day dress. She was in need of clothes until her own trunk arrived. Next, she found a butcher shop for meat, then a grocery for supplies to share with her dog: barley, potatoes, canned vegetables, cheese, and bread. The heavy-jawed woman who ran the store offered, "You might see the City Fish Market for offal. Dogs love it."

When Emma was on her way back past the dental office, Otis stepped outside onto the boardwalk. He looked both ways then leaned toward her and spoke lowly. "It is true, Emma? You are not here because you changed your mind about my proposal?"

"I have not, Otis. I simply had nowhere else to go to start a business, free from worry of Cutter."

"Molly is a pleasure. She suits me very well."

"I'm sure she does." Emma was embarrassed that Otis felt a need to explain himself.

"Then I have an extra office here you could rent. You should not be with strangers. There are many ruffians here. Molly is willing to receive Dr. Emma's clientele, and we could use the lease money."

They struck a deal standing beside the muddy street. "Now the boarder has become the landlord!" Emma said in delight.

"That's decided then. I am glad I am not what you are seeking, but I'm glad you found us nonetheless," Otis said, solemnly touching the back of her hand. "I will always hold fond memories of the Prescott Boarding House." He turned and went back into his practice.

She had her office. And a new friend in Molly. If the truth were told, and it did not appear to be her day for telling truths, she preferred Molly to Otis. She was pleased to have such a strong barrier, in case she ever really had considered marriage to the dentist. Which she hadn't. Not really. Not since Sev anyway. The day was bleak with a fine cold mist, but she hardly noticed as she made her final stop at the bank. She had an account in Seattle and wanted funds moved to Port Angeles. Emma was not a rich woman, but had inherited enough from her mother to be comfortable for several months while she built her business. Now she was nearly out of coins as well as paper notes. And one couldn't live on gold nuggets alone. It was better she keep their existence to herself.

* * *

Emma's head was buzzing with plans for her office when she returned to the Axton house. She went to her room, which looked devoid of personal possessions. The meagerness of her wardrobe amused her; it had all fit in one drawer of the commodious chest. She looked forward to the new dress from Molly and the arrival of her trunk.

It wasn't clothing she wanted most. She wanted her medical equipment and textbooks. These treasures were also in her trunk. The few remaining supplies from her medical bag were nearly useless from their dunking in saltwater. Only a few precious teas and tinctures were preserved within bottles and tins. The morphine, her gauze, and bandaging were gone. She would look for an apothecary here, but didn't expect to like it even if she found one. Most were run by pharmacists who didn't actually make their own medicines anymore. Their shelves were stocked with pre-made tablets and capsules.

"Who knows what is in those prefabricated pills?" Emma muttered to herself in the tiny gilt mirror mounted on the wall. She liked a trained pharmacist who custom-made with pure ingredients. "No snake oil, thank you very much." Emma was aware that, like many new practitioners, she showed symptoms of being a know-it-all, even though her mettle was largely untested.

She went to the kitchen with her grocery purchases. A right to use it had come with her rent. It was so clean, aromatic, and bright, it reminded her of home. She cooked a pot of barley, boiled the meat scraps in it, and added chunks of bread to make a gruel for Koira. While the combination bubbled on the stove, she sat at the kitchen table with Betty Axton's four-pound Montgomery Ward catalog.

"Monkey Ward!" chirped Birdie, coming through the back door, home from school. "Are you getting something fun?"

"Yes. Towels, sheets, trays, cups, and bottles for my new office."

A bowl haircut did little for the child's chubby face as it fell into a tragedy mask. "That's not fun, Miss Emma. That's boring."

"Not to me. Want to go feed Big Puppy then take him for a walk?"

By the time they had gone to the shed and fed Koira, the child was not up to a walk. She had started to wheeze. Emma remembered her cough from the morning. It now sounded dry and deep. They went into the house to find Betty kneading bread in the kitchen with a hearty slap and punch. Koira tiptoed in behind them, silent and stealthy as an enormous feral cat.

"Oh, not again," Betty said when she heard Birdie's wheeze. She stopped kneading and immediately wiped her hands on her apron.

"Does this happen often?" Emma asked, as the child gasped.

"Put on your coat, Birdie. We'll see Dr. Obermayer." Betty removed her apron.

"I don't want to go, Mama." Birdie protested.

Betty patted her hair while saying, "Get your coat now, young miss."

To Emma, who was donning the apron to take over with the bread, Betty said, "It happens more often in the winter. 'Merely a spot of asthma,' the local sawbones calls it. Makes me feel like I worry for nothing. God forbid it's consumption."

"What does the doctor do for it?" Punch, slap, roll, punch.

"A breathing treatment in his office with a device he calls a Pulverisateur. "

"Does such a nebulizer work?"

"I guess. But she hates it. And her problem always comes back. Why are you asking?"

"You know I am an eclectic physician. I think I can help. See your doctor. When you come home, I'll explain."

It sounded worse than 'a spot of asthma' to Emma. It sounded worse than that. Slap, punch, punch. She set the bread in a bowl to rise, covering it with a towel. Then she turned to get Koira from the shed, but he was directly behind her. "Goodness! Did Birdie let you in? Well, come along."

They walked into the woods on a rugged trail. The forest curved in an arch around the little town, an endless green tide rolling up to the mountains. It smelled wonderful, the damp air redolent with fir and cedar.

Koira viewed all those trees as dog heaven, and he went off to lift a leg on as many as possible. Emma relished the opportunity to kick some of the road mud off her boots and skirt hem; the path under the trees was firmer and less churned with foot traffic. She had not gone far before finding a fallen log which nursed several young hemlock trees as it decayed. Water hemlock was highly toxic, but many parts of Western hemlock trees were marvelous for healing. Emma stripped the tender bark from lower branches, then pried up chunks of resin with Cutter's knife.

Cutter. You blight. I hope you are dead.

Emma knew she should be uncomfortable with that thought. What a thing for a physician to contemplate! But she was so tired of his visage turning up like the proverbial bad penny in crowds and surreal dreams.

She sighed. Seeing Koira rolling joyfully on something smelly, she said, "Koira, I am becoming a hardened pioneer lady. You, on the other hand, remain a ridiculous critter."

Emma would have liked new green tips of the hemlock branches, but it was too early for them to have formed. Something to harvest in the spring. The bark would take time to dry before becoming a tea. But the resin she could use now.

Back in the kitchen, she warmed it to a consistency of molasses, picking out any bits of bark, cone or impurities. As it warmed, she added rubbing alcohol and some of Betty's bear grease. She mixed it thoroughly into a salve, wishing she had bees wax but could do without.

The bread dough was in the oven when Betty and Birdie returned. "I'm sorry, Emma. We had to wait. Doc did a breathing treatment but said there was not much more he could do, and that I should carry out such treatments myself at home."

She sat at the table as Birdie went to cuddle Big Puppy. Betty's face fell into wrinkles that appeared deeper than before.

Emma said, "I will take the dog out if..."

"No. He makes her happy." Tears trembled in Betty's eyes. "I swear Emma, I feel like I was fired by that damn doctor for lack of cause. He has no understanding of a mother's concern."

"I have some things you can try, Betty, if you would like."

"Dr. Obermayer said you'd say that. In fact, he had harsh things to say about eclectics in general."

"That may be because too many of us have called too many of him quacks."

Betty managed a grin and patted Emma's hand. "Thank you for that, Emma. I needed a bit of humor."

"If you are willing, give this a try." Emma handed her a tin of the salve. "At bedtime, rub some on Birdie's throat. And tomorrow I will brew a special tea. Hemlock and consumptive's weed. They can both relieve inflammation in the throat. Whether it is asthma or another chronic respiratory issue, they will help Birdie breathe easier. It is not a cure but will give her relief."

In the week that followed, Birdie responded well to the tea, as long as it contained a dollop of honey. She was served a cup whenever she began to cough.

"I have a small cache of dried leaves from the consumptive's weed. We can make more in the spring," Emma explained to Betty. "We'll use hemlock tea to see us through. It's not as good, but once the healing starts, she'll likely need it less often."

Confined to the house for a few days, Birdie taught Big Puppy to sit, stay, and wear a doll bonnet perched atop his head, tied round with a large bow at his neck. They spent enough time together that Emma began to worry whether the child could be allergic to dogs. But Birdie's cough did not increase, while her laughter did. Koira wormed his way into every room of the house and every heart.

Emma taught Betty how to use a nebulizer, even obtaining necessary chemicals from the doctor. She wanted to meet him and see if they could establish a degree of trust in each other.

It might have been easier if he hadn't looked exactly like engravings of Ebenezer Scrooge. What little hair he had wafted in the air like a tuft of baby duck feathers. He wore a long coat with a stained vest. Its top buttoned tight over a sunken chest but gave way over his rounded belly. Wire-rimmed bifocals perched on his nose tip, and his mouth was a tight little pout even in repose.

Dr. Obermayer's opening gambit did nothing to endear the physical physician to the eclectic physician. "We don't need a petticoat peddling old-fangled ideas around here."

Since she might have need of this rattlecap in the days ahead, Emma tried for sweetness as an offense. "I am helping Mrs. Axton do what you suggested, good sir, teaching her to treat her daughter at home in order to save your time for serious issues. I am requesting supplies from you. I intend you no competition."

"See it stays that way."

"Miserable clyster-pipe," she said to the universe-at-large on her way home, using slang for a doctor that she had never said aloud before and would likely never use again.

Nothing was said by Betty about payment for Emma's services, not exactly. But Emma was invited to dine at the Axton's table every evening. It was her first experience with payment in trade. It was not the Seattle way, but Emma learned it was a staple in the Port Angeles community.

Emma cleaned her office space, commissioned shelving, a cabinet, and an exam table to be built. She purchased a desk from a CPA whose assistant left town with embezzled money. When the weather allowed, Emma walked the woods, harvesting what she could during the winter hours. So far it had been a winter of very little snow, but torrents of rain.

She explored her new town door-to-door when, after four days of sun, the muddy streets turned dusty, and the boardwalks were dry of puddles. Shopkeepers like the grocer began to recognize her or at least the very large dog that parked himself outside when Emma came inside.

The establishments that concerned her were in a U-shape from the waterfront, south on Lincoln, west on Front, and north on Laurel until the street ended on Morris dock. From the dock she could see steamers enter and leave the harbor and the many mills at work. The air smelled of ocean and fir pitch, especially when the incoming tide rose over exposed waste flats under the docks. The Port Angeles downtown was a tiny area for one used to Seattle, but it served her purposes rather better than she had at first thought. Goods not locally available could be ordered from Seattle or back east and were delivered regularly on the freight steamers.

The town businesses included livery and a blacksmith. Hotel, laundry, fish market, general merchandise, grocer, and clothing stores. A pharmacy she actually liked, two restaurants, hardware store that also featured arms and ammunition. And, counting them as places she would never need, there were two taverns and at least one brothel.

About the brothel, she would be proven wrong.

CHAPTER TWELVE

Port Angeles, Strait of Juan de Fuca
January 23, 1904

At last, a letter from Lillian arrived. Emma almost skipped to her room, giddy to read it. She flounced onto her bed, carefully opening the thick envelope. To her joy, folded inside Lillian's letter, was the one from Severin. Since it was the older of the two, Emma opened it first. At least that's the reason she gave herself.

January 13
My dear Emma,
I have just left you on Union Wharf to find my way to Victoria. I will locate a hotel when I get there (hopefully tonight) then check in to the inquest on the morrow. All crew members who survived the Clallam *have been asked to appear here or in the United States or both. After my duty is dealt with, I will travel to Sidney to visit my parents and brother. It is but a carriage or boat ride from Victoria.*
I have discovered that you and I were not the last two survivors found alive after the Clallam *tragedy. A crewman (known as an oiler) drifted all night in a waterlogged craft. He was picked up by the* Sea Lion, *one of the rescue boats making a return trip. The poor man was in plain sight of the Smith Island lighthouse when we were there, but helplessly adrift with no way to attract our attention.*

January 14

I made it to Victoria, and will mail this on my way to the inquest. If you did not see the article in The Morning Leader *in Port Townsend, prepare yourself. You were mentioned as a possible survivor, but by first name only. One of the men on the lighthouse tender must have spoken to a reporter about us.*

I am sure that the villain who stalked you died in the depths on that horrifying night, but do be cautious, my dear girl. Whether he is dead or alive, be careful in all things. I have grown a new nerve where your welfare is concerned. Leaving you on that wharf was tantamount to leaving a piece of myself in my wake.

I hope this letter finds you well. Please write to me care of general delivery in Sidney, Vancouver Island, British Columbia, Canada. I will continue to reach you at Prescott Boarding House until advised otherwise. It is my wish that, by the time you read this, you have found a safe and pleasant home.

With affection,
Severin

Emma's heart danced merrily. Sev missed her, at least on the day he wrote this letter. Maybe she had faded in his memory since then, but maybe she remained as clear to him as he did to her. Next her heart thumped with the same old fear. Her name had appeared in the press. If Cutter was alive, and if he saw it...well, then what? How would he know where she had gone? Nobody had seen her leave with the Klallam tribe.

Had they?

She set Severin's letter aside on her bed to unfold the one from Lillian. It started merry as a birdsong, so glad was Lillian that Emma was alive. Then it settled down, asking for details of the shipwreck and all that had happened. Next, Lillian turned to business, updating the running of the boarding house, the purchase of new locks for the front windows, and their first new boarder, a clock maker. Finally, Lillian introduced a subject that further increased the patter of Emma's heart.

My mother is besotted with Mr. Crogan as a choice in matrimony for me. She is advancing this agenda like a child campaigning for a new toy. The woman is often full of silly ideas, but I must confess, my dear friend, I also find Timothy to be quite the fellow. I seem to be experiencing what I believe is called a crush. Oh, how I wish you were here so I could discuss my secret flame with you. I have no one else to tell! Would you allow us to continue with the boarding house if we were Mr. and Mrs. Timothy Crogan? Do you suppose he might ask an old bit of mutton such as myself? I am approaching thirty, after all.

Enough about me. You will have seen I enclosed a letter from Mr. Severin Eronen. Be honest with me Emma...you read his letter before mine, did you not? Was it chocked full of sweet nothings? Loving whispers in your ear? Are you besotted with this stranger? Tell me more!

I close now to prepare the evening meal. Timothy wants a word with you so he has written on the back of this sheet. He was not allowed to read the front, and I kept watch on him to assure his compliance. My letter is for your eyes only, my true friend.

Warmly,
Lillian

Emma, grinning like a Cheshire cat, turned the sheet over. On the back, printed in letters dark and heavy:

Keep yer chin up and give the rascals hell. Timothy

By the time she read her letters through a second and a third time, Emma's cheeks hurt from smiling. Going to the kitchen table, Emma immediately answered them all.

January 23
Dear Lillian,
Your letter arrived today along with the note from Timothy and letter from Severin Eronen. Opening these treasures far outshines a Christmas morn. I am so blessed with your friendship. Now then. There is much to tell. I have a fine new place to live with a couple and their wonderful little girl, aptly named Birdie. In addition, an office for my medical practice is nearly ready to open. It is housed in the same business as the dentist Otis Combes and managed by his wife, Molly. Yes, Otis is married!

Emma wrote at length about the town, the new dress that Molly was making for her, and how she had traveled with natives from one town to the next, in order to stay under the radar if Cutter were still around.

The girl's name is Willa, and she is of the Klallam tribe. She shared medicinal plants with me and explained much about the natives here. Willa and Molly are both my age, but so very different. They cannot replace my dear Lillian, but at least I am not lonely for female company.

Now, about company of the masculine variety. I cannot but hope that Timothy sees the wisdom in your mother's sales pitches. You are a genuine find, as is he, I am sure as eggs is eggs of that. Please keep me advised on that front. As to Severin, yes, we spent time together after the shipwreck. He was a help to me through that sorrow, and I to him. I like to think a romance was planted, but he has commitments to another that will keep it from growing. There cannot be more to our relationship unless and until he deals with that.

I will enclose a note for Timothy. Please tell him not to worry about me. Write soon, and count on a deluge of mail from me.
Your frontier friend,
Emma

Emma composed her message to Timothy and tucked it inside the envelope to Lillian. She also enclosed a tuft of Koira's thick black hair.

January 23
My Dear Timothy,
*   I have a dog named Koira! He is a very large fellow, one whose jowls could close around the neck of the most scurrilous of outlaws, even one such as Cutter. I feel it safe to say he is as strong and loyal as my good friend, Timothy, although he does not give me as many orders. As you can tell from the tress enclosed, he is a gentleman with a proper head of hair, if you don't mind my mentioning the matter. If I can't have you to watch over me in this uncivilized land, then Koira will do. Be assured that together, my dog and I will give the rascals hell.*
*   Fondly,*
*   Emma*

She did not tell Lillian about her night with Severin, about the touch of his skin, the weight and aroma of his strong body upon hers. She could not write such things. Besides, Lillian might not understand such reckless behavior, having not experienced firsthand the sort of traumatic ordeal the couple had been through. How could she comprehend the need to cling to each other?

Emma was well aware of her own plainness and was not convinced that she was more than a moment of comfort to Sev. Would the correspondent who wrote that letter a week ago still be as affectionate today, after time had its cooling effect? Emma doubted he was still factoring her into his future, and she had no desire to embarrass either him or herself by assuming too much. She found herself reining in her emotions as she wrote to him now.

January 23

Dear Severin,

What a delight to receive your letter of January 13. It wandered for a week, making its way from Seattle to my new home here in Port Angeles, arriving today; if you choose to keep it, see my return address on the envelope.

Thank you for the update on your progress. I presume you may be finished with the inquest by now. If you communicate again, please tell me about that as I am, of course, curious regarding the outcome. Has the captain been blamed for the misadventure? From what I read in the newspapers, I fear he will be.

I will be opening my medical office soon and have established friendships with two women already. The town is small and exudes frontier roughness, but it has treated me most kindly in these first few days. Koira, the loving Newfoundland dog, stays at my side. No, I have heard no more of Cutter, other than in my dreams. Perhaps he is merely a ghost by now.

I trust you are enjoying your visit with your family, and if your bride-to-be has arrived, that the arrangement is pleasing to you. I assume you will continue to sail these scary seas on which we live, you in one country and I another.

With regards,

Emma

There. Not loving, but not not loving. Restrained, but not formal. Informative, but not dwelling on shared history. It was the best she could do for now. But late that night, after she had mailed her correspondence, Emma lay awake thinking of all the words she would like to have written to this man who was spending a surprising amount of time in her brain.

* * *

At breakfast, a young lad appeared at the Axton door, delivering a note from Molly. She wrote that a woman had stopped to see the doctor and gone away disappointed that the office was not open. This woman requested that Emma come to the aid of her friend at Angel's Parlor, south on Laurel at the mouth of an alley. But Emma should know, Molly wrote, that this was a brothel. And Emma must come to the dentist's office for lunch to tell Molly all about it.

What on earth would a Port Angeles 'Angel' want from her? No sooner had Emma's noggin formulated the question, than it popped out the answer. This woman wanted Emma's medical help, of course.

"I may have my first patient!" Emma said aloud.

"I am your first patient," Birdie replied, clarifying the situation before she gulped the last of the disagreeable hemlock tea.

"Well, yes, but you are more family than client," Emma said. "However, I stand corrected. I have my second patient."

Emma knew little about the prostitute trade but had great curiosity. Still, she was loath to ask Axe lest he knew a little too much. She decided to go to Angel's Parlor immediately. Women's issues were a great part of her education at school. Besides, a new practitioner couldn't be too choosy. A prostitute was at least likely to understand the concept of payment for services rendered.

Emma had restocked what supplies she could at the local pharmacy, including gauze, bandages, and the small amount of morphine she used for Severin and herself during the *Clallam* disaster. She steadfastly refused patent medicines containing opiates or cocaine, all readily available in the pharmacy or through catalogs. There was a time not long ago that opium and a syringe could be purchased from Sears. It made the new eclectic physician shudder with outrage.

Emma wore the new dress from Molly, wanting to look her most professional, although the rain slicker from Lillian's brother did little to enhance her image. The brothel's location was set just back from the waterfront so sailors had a short walk to it, and loggers would find it a convenient journey from the woods. Either group would likely be too drunk and too eager for peak performance by the time they arrived, Emma imagined.

The house was little different from the ones around it except for the rather large hitching post outside and the red draperies at the front window. Peeking in, Emma thought the parlor looked like just that...a formal room with comfortable, if aging, Victorian furnishings. Naked ladies and lust-crazed men were not strewn from ottoman to sideboard. Maybe it was simply too early in the day.

"Do I go to the front door as though I were one of the clientele? Or slink around to the back?" she asked Koira.

Koira didn't answer.

Emma decided on the front and marched up the wide step to knock.

The door was opened by the biggest human being Emma had ever seen. He was easily the size of two normal men, maybe three. His long dark hair and skin tone made her think of the Klallam natives, but he was far too large. He would fit in no canoe that she could picture. His pant legs appeared tight and printed in a crazy pattern. Then she realized he had no long pants. His legs were actually bare and fully tattooed from his shorts to his knees. As for the rest, he was covered in a tent-like dyed shirt.

Emma might have backed away from such a surprise, but she had to grab Koira at that exact moment to keep the dog from lunging at this colossus. "Koira! Bad dog! Stop this and stay," she snapped over the racket of the growling Newfie. So much for her professional appearance. Holding him tightly, she said, "I am Emm, ah, Dr. Emma Prescott, come at the insistence of a resident here."

The mountain of man did not move until an old woman's voice behind him called, "Awa. Let her in."

Awa moved back a few inches, enough for Emma to enter while Koira stayed where he'd been told, loudly grumbling his displeasure.

If the man was the biggest human Emma had ever seen, the woman was the oldest outside a death bed. Wrinkly ruts covered her face as thoroughly as Awa's tattoos covered his thighs. Her elfin frame made her seem frail.

"I am Angel," the old woman said with a smile, reaching for Emma's hand.

Surely, this was not a prostitute! A feather might fell her, she was so tiny, although her manner was spry enough.

The merriment in the crone's laugh was catching. "No, I am no longer for hire, my dear Doctor. Men would rather ride a broom than me these days. Angel just happens to be my real name, believe it or not. I own and run this establishment, having plied the trade many decades along the Barbary coast." Here, her voice turned steely. "You are willing to treat my whores more civilly than that pestilence, Dr. Obermayer?"

So the good doctor had made himself popular here, too. Starting her business might be easier than Emma had hoped, what with the way he treated patients. "I work with botanicals as well as medical solutions of traditional physicians. I am a graduate of the Eclectic Medical College of Missouri. I will do my best by you and your...staff."

"Good then." The ancient reached high up to pat the giant's shoulder. "Awa, she appears to be safe."

He burst into a wide grin, bowed, and spoke with an accent unknown to Emma. "Proud to meet you, Dr. Emma. I do startle people, which is the point of the man at the door of an establishment such as this, don't you know. I apologize to you and that big hairy brute out there for giving you both a fright."

Emma could not put that tenor voice with this enormous body. "You are...not from here? You look somehow..."

"Samoa is my native land. South Pacific. But I learned English from Atlantic whalers I sailed with for years. Long story. I daresay, they are responsible for the accent and much else about my life."

Emma felt a lack of knowledge even greater than her understanding of the local natives. She wanted to know more. But Angel interrupted.

"Come to the back, Doctor. See what you might be able to do for Ruby." The tiny madam led the way down a corridor.

Three girls watched from doorways onto the hall. Each was scruffy, red-eyed. *It must be too early in the day for men but my arrival has wakened them,* Emma thought. One of the fallen angels touched her arm as she passed by.

"Help our Ruby, Doc."

The madam led her to a small room with a bed, lamp, nightstand, and very little else. Emma half expected to see the results of a prostitute's use of mercury or arsenic with vinegar. They were known to inject such vile concoctions with vaginal syringes to induce abortion.

But Ruby's issue was not self-medication. The adolescent in the bed had been beaten, severely so. As Emma viewed the unconscious young face, she could not help but gasp. "A customer did this to her?"

Angel nodded. "Goes with the trade, I am sorry to say. He will not be allowed in this house again."

"You've alerted the police?"

"He's one of the police. We call him Billy, short for Billy Club. If I complain too much, they'll close us down. If I keep still, they'll allow Awa to keep that bugger away. Unspoken agreement between us."

"Appalling." Emma set to work, first reeling from the girl's breath. "She is unconscious with alcohol?"

"The only pain relief we have to give her," Angel answered.

"It's just as well." Emma started by cleaning then stitching a ragged cut below the girl's left eye. Fortunately, the socket and cheekbone seemed intact. Time would tell whether Ruby's sight would be the same. Next, Emma checked her mouth, looking for the cause of the bleeding there. Two broken teeth, at least.

When Emma unlaced the girl's nightshirt, she revealed dreadful bruises from Ruby's breasts on down her abdomen. "Surely, someone heard this happening!"

Angel replied, "He gagged her. And, my dear naive doctor, most whores do not tell on each other's trade." Emma could see, for all the madam's bravado, a tear was working its way down the rugged topography of the old woman's face.

Emma applied poultices for pain and left a tincture the girl could use for the bruising. "I'll be back tomorrow to check for infection. Give her these drops of morphine when she awakens."

Angel thanked her and handed her a few coins.

"Keep men away from her until she heals," Emma ordered.

"Prostitutes can ill-afford time off, and Ruby is a favorite," Angel said. "I assume you are new to the ways of this trade, Doctor. It is not an easy one."

"Yes. Well. I'll check in on her tomorrow." Emma wanted to shriek but wasn't sure at who...the madam, the girl, the man, society in general.

"If you are willing to come when we have the need, I will call on you again in the future."

So the girls of Angel's Parlor became Dr. Emma's first paying clientele. She no longer felt joyful about her new patient. These women saddened her, but they needed her, and she needed them. She arrived at the dentist office having walked at such a furious pace that Koira had to trot to keep up. Emma wanted the ear of a friend, and Molly had asked for it.

"He beat her, Molly. He thrashed her with a truncheon. And her private parts are torn." Emma's outrage found outlet in her friend's kitchen as the two prepared the luncheon stew.

Otis joined them for the meal, and Emma told him a less graphic version of the occurrence. "Her mouth was bloody, and she appears to have lost a tooth or two. I suggested to her, ah, boss that she see you when she is up and around."

He nodded. "I will see her, of course. But we must take care, Emma. Especially you."

"What do you mean?"

"I have no competition to my craft of dentistry. But Dr. Obermayer is a wheel in this town, one who will need some grease for you."

"I have already crossed the man regarding my landlady's daughter."

"Don't let him find a way to undercut you. About Angel's Parlor, for instance. He could well twist your

ministration to a certain level of society, making you appear
a lower class practitioner."

"How would he dare? Who is he to dictate to me or to
deny aid to any level of society?" Emma felt the acid taste of
fury for the second time this day.

Otis held up his hands as if they could turn her tirade
aside. "You asked me for advice and guidance with matters
on this frontier, Emma, and I am giving it. Don't allow
Obermayer the chance to end your career before you start.
Tread carefully around him."

When Otis left for his downstairs office, Emma sulked.
"I feel like Otis thinks I'm a prostitute because I cared for
one. That I've lowered myself."

"Piffle. He thinks no such thing, and you know it. He's
been a businessman a long time and knows the importance
of smoothing the waters."

"I know, Molly. I truly don't doubt he is correct. But
why are things always so hard? We fight for everything. To
go to school, to be safe, to vote, to work at what we want..."

Molly snorted. "Like trying to be a female tailor, you
mean? You tell me."

Emma knew her friend had a difficult journey ahead.
"You made me a lovely frock, Molly. Wouldn't dressmaking
be an easier goal?"

"Maybe. But it's not what I do. I know far more about
the different body shapes for men, how to cut and construct
their garments. Besides, there are so many more men than
women out here. When the time is right, I will make suits
for two or three men, hoping they will model them around
town."

"A fine scheme, Molly. You are clever at this. Maybe
you could help me with an ad for the paper."

Molly was still planning big. "I know! Let's host a party
for the new dentist, the new eclectic, and the new tailor. It

will be a sort of spring fling for a growing town. Drawings for a free dental checkup. A free selection of your restorative teas. An alteration from me. Everyone will come. Even that sour old doctor." Her eyes narrowed as she schemed. "We'll choose him for one of my models. He'll be eating out of our hands in no time.

* * *

Four days later, two letters arrived from Severin. Both were forwarded to Port Angeles from Seattle, so Emma knew he had not yet received her letter to him.

...I heard some of the testimony today. It was very sad, reminding me of things I would prefer to forget. One of my shipmates recounted fighting with a girl who was determined not to get into a lifeboat. But it was the captain's orders for all the women and children. He had to do his duty. At that point in his testimony, he broke down and cried. He will feel responsible for the girl's loss for the rest of his life.

I have never believed in miracles, Emma. But you onboard, dressed as a boy? It saved your life! Having you in my arms is reason enough for me to concede to the miraculous.

His second letter told more of the trial and his belief that the captain might be blamed for the whole thing.

...People seem especially suspicious of his decisions because he is an officer in the Puget Sound Navigation Company. It is implied he had more financial interest in saving the boat than the passengers. I have known Captain Roberts for years, never doubted him. It is difficult for me to believe he would be guilty of such a thing.

Are you well, dear Emma? I am so eager to hear from you. I wonder where you are."

It was early February when a third letter arrived. This time it came directly to her, not forwarded from Seattle. So Severin had received her first communication. And he was upset.

You sound so distant, Emma, more like a stranger than the girl of my heart. Have I offended you? Do you not trust in me? Perhaps you are shy to put your feelings in words. Please tell me you remember our shared distress in the deep waters, our mutual salvation, our time together with all the emotion for me that I feel for you.

Emma sighed. She'd been wrong. She did matter to Severin. She was more than a bond of sorrow or a night of infatuation. Once again, she had misjudged a man. Was it too late to recover the territory she had lost? "I am truly no good at this romance nincompoopery, Koira. Dogs are much easier to understand than men."

The Newfie looked at her with affection, bashed his tail on the floor and drooled from his wide mouth and pink tongue. Emma sighed again. "But speaking as a former manager of a boarding house with men, dogs are messier."

February 4
My dearest Sev,
My trunk arrived today; it was in my room at the Axton home when I returned from my office. It is marvelous to have my clothes. I put on a favorite dress immediately, one I wonder if you would like. I must admit, I am very tired of a boy's slicker, so the advent of my wool cape is like the arrival of an old friend.

I can now consult my textbooks and medicines to find solutions for particular issues that have arisen with my earliest patients. You might be surprised to know that Dr. Emma is now

*the physician for our local house of ill repute. I tell you that in case
my avocation might shock you from your interest in me.*

*Sev, do not think I have withdrawn my affection. What I felt,
I continue to feel, but I have no wish to assume more than you can
give. I think about you, wondering if you would like it here. But
then I remember your intended bride, and I must not go any
further in the direction of coveting that girl's promised husband.*

*You know I have been married and have suffered the sorrow
of that mistake. I don't want such a misstep for you. I cherish my
time with you, but I have no more claim on you.*

Tell me you understand.

Emma

* * *

Oregon Penitentiary was old, diseased, and violent
long before Harry Tracy escaped it in 1902. Now it was
Goodwyn Lewis' turn to dwell behind the fourteen-foot
concrete walls.

The men who had busted down Cutter's door, shortly
after his return from the *Clallam* disaster, were federal
marshals. They'd read his name on the medical list of
survivors, wanted him for an Oregon train robbery, plucked
him out of Seattle, and dropped him in the Salem cesspool.

By the time he arrived, the use of flogging and the
tortuous Oregon boot shackles were by and large things of
the past. But bruising sprays of water, guards armed with
canes, and inmate accidents in the prison's foundry were the
order-of-the-day. Malaria, chronic rheumatism, catarrh,
and body wounds were rampant.

Cutter was not at his best when they nabbed him,
recovering from his bruises and wounds acquired during
the shipwreck. In the early days of incarceration, he suffered
many infections and developed a chronic cough.

What kept him alive were dreams of Emma and revenge. It was no longer the gold he chased; by now it was at the bottom of the sea, or she had spent it, or at least she'd no longer carry it with her. It was the bitch herself that he wanted. She became the source of all evil, far larger than life. She was a ghost-thief who stole everything from him. The idea of her consumed him, enraged and terrified him. He was no longer sure if he chased her or she chased him.

He was miserable, beaten down, and overworked. Still, if he ever recovered, he would escape. Oregon Penitentiary, with its crumbling structure, scalable walls, and outside work programs was a sieve for those determined enough to go free.

Cutter might be demented. But he was nothing if not determined.

CHAPTER THIRTEEN

Port Angeles, Strait of Juan de Fuca
March, 1904

To my pioneer friend, Emma,

Well, it has happened! I am to be Mrs. Crogan in May. Wait until the suffragettes at Louella Braxton's house hear about that! The proposal was the outcome of an evening of confession on the parts of both Timothy and me. After dinner, my mother and brother retired early. Our boarder works on his clocks in his room in the evenings. He says he hopes to invent a wind-free wristwatch. Our new residents, two young ladies you really must meet, move in tomorrow.

That left Timothy, me, and a bottle of sherry alone in the parlor. Possibly he was urged onward for fear we'd never have a moment alone again (I wonder if the new automobiles I see in the Seattle streets will lead to more alone time for couples; if so, no wonder they're so popular).

Back to my main subject. Timothy asked me a rather personal question about why I was not married.

I explained as best I could, about women of what the press calls the New West. How we prefer to establish ourselves, not merely be extensions of our husbands. While some still feel marriage and bearing babies is the only point of being a woman, the New West allows us additional options, regardless of our families or pasts.

'So that's not just a newshound's tommyrot?" Timothy asked, and of course, I set him straight. He must understand how important a right to vote is to me, and how that belief has intimidated the average man. Besides, my mother and little brother are in my care, which is a distinct deterrent to the matrimonial process.

When I reached my sermon's end, I asked him the same question. As it happens, he was married in Ireland. He saw his wife and child clubbed to death in a riot, overrun by soldiers. Timothy was a wanted man, a notorious rebel. He sailed from Dublin to save what was left of his life and has never returned. He had not intended to consider marriage again.

But then he asked for my hand! I would blush to tell you what all he said, but it included, "I liked a New West woman when I met Emma. I loved a New West woman when I met you."

Mother is thrilled beyond reason but requests at least a three-month engagement so there is time for the things she will enjoy, things like wedding showers, planning the service, choosing the flowers and songs. I care little for that balderdash, but she is happy. Timothy and I can wait for the ceremony, but I confess to you, my discreet friend, I am grateful his private quarters in the cellar are so far from the main bedrooms in this house. Possibly I will need one of your personal ointments or creams!

Your shameless blushing bride,
Lillian

Emma laughed aloud. Personal, indeed! Lillian had always been free with her thoughts and opinions. It put off those with more traditional sensibilities, but her openness delighted Emma.

Lillian!
What wonderful news. You must congratulate the Irish charmer for me. I hope he is up for the open-minded helpmate with

whom he is about to join forces. You will have such fun years together. Oh, how happy I am for you both.

Things are well here. I am in my office most days now, receiving new clients who are slowly finding me as my reputation spreads from mouth to ear. A hairdresser gave my skincare advice for acne a try, and now she recommends me to the ladies whose tresses she styles. The prostitutes seek my tincture of sweetroot for their candida. I must buy it dried to make my product; in the summer I will harvest my own. It tastes of anise so is far more pleasant to take orally than to inject insane concoctions into one's private places. The easiest harvest in this wintry month is evergreen bark and foliage, therefore I make things like cedar tincture to apply to warts. I will be ready if a toad needs my help!

A man has yet to seek my services, men being more conservative about female practitioners than women are about men. It is as well. I do not want to poke Dr. Obermayer in the eye by taking his patients away.

What manner of wedding gift shall I purchase for my friends? A stump from the saw mills cut into an enormous bell? A crate of clams? A haunch of elk? Shopping is peculiar in Port Angeles, so I must give this great thought.

Before writing to Severin, Emma reread his most recent letter to her. He'd told her more about the *Clallam* inquest as well as his visit with his family. And he had given her cause to fret, which was already her natural inclination.

...The Canadian officials seem unforgiving and eager to blame captain, crew, vessel, and ship inspectors alike for missing safety equipment, bad decisions, and poor communication between bridge and engine room. Inquests in the United States seem to be more understanding, for better or worse. There appears to be agreement on your side of the Strait that, yes there was faulty decision-making, but in the face of that, everyone did the best they

*could. I do not know where Captain Roberts is at the moment, but
if I were he, I would depart Canada for the states. I believe he has
a better chance to avoid a manslaughter charge there.*

This phrase stopped Emma as it had the first time she'd
read Sev's letter. Manslaughter? The man was wrong about
lowering the lifeboats, but hadn't it been what he believed
was right? Surely the captain was paying enough penance
in a living hell over that decision.

*...To another subject that is of equal import to you and me, if
not more so. I am staying with my parents and brother Jorin.
Jorin, now twenty, is the son I am not. He stayed with forestry
while I went to sea. He learned Finnish which I resisted. He breaks
few rules while I seem determined to upset the household. He is a
homebody while I am a traveler. He is handsome, and I am not.*

*I have spoken to Jorin, and we have shaken hands on a plan.
The girl who is presently at sea, coming for me, will become his
bride instead! He is an altogether better mate for her. And I will
give them a small monthly stipend for the first two years to help
him start his own logging crew, an operation which is his dream.*

*Is this not a fabulous plan, good for all parties? Yet, I must
admit, I am nervous of presenting it to my parents which Jorin
and I intend to do this evening. They will reject the idea as
inappropriate for a younger brother to wed before an older, but in
the end, they will see the wisdom.*

*Emma, I think about you on the other side of the raging
Strait, a country away but so close. I imagine you, professional in
your new office, laughing with your friend Molly, and throwing
sticks for your silly black dog. In the excitement of so much
newness, do not forget,*

> *Yours truly,*
> *Sev*

This letter created enough panic in Emma that she needed the calming effect of one of her own teas. Was this crazy Canadian changing his life on behalf of a woman with whom he'd spent less than a week? She felt she could love him, but she had felt that for Ronan. Even if Sev negotiated his way out of an arranged marriage, did he think she was ready to negotiate her way into one?

Am I?

Emma took Koira for a long walk by the new brewery building on Tumwater and threw sticks for him. They cut back to the waterfront and watched the steamer *Whatcom* load passengers bound for Everett. Then she returned home and began to write. The words of her reply were as honest as she could make them. Sev had made up his mind, but she had not.

Dear Sev,

First, let me say that you are very handsome, so I shall hear no more of that. Otherwise, I might yearn to meet your brother!

By now, you and Jorin have spoken with your parents regarding your intended. I do hope the conversation ended in the best interests of you all. I also hope the girl has an opportunity to express her opinion on the matter. Does she have a name? I would prefer to stop calling her 'the girl.'

Severin, many words are difficult for me to say out loud, and even more so on paper. Women, at least in America if not in Canada, are raised keeping secrets and hiding true emotions. I was luckier than most to have a mother who had little difficulty speaking her mind. Still, it is challenging to set society's training aside. But I believe I owe it to you.

I came to the frontier to escape a man stalking me, no other reason. I liked living in the Prescott Boarding House and would have opened an office there. However, I find to my surprise, I am loving it here on the brink of the wild, the adventure and scope of it. It is so fresh and new to me. Possibilities seem endless.

While you have never mentioned the word marriage, I can't help but think you have it in mind. And I must caution that I would not make a man a very traditional wife after I have tasted the freedom of this place. Could you picture yourself here, on the edge of the continent in a country that is not your own?

I adored meeting you, talking with you, sharing our sorrow as well as the pleasure of that night in the...well, you understand. Still, you know so little about me or I about you. What are your hobbies, how do you feel about the vote for women, what is your religious belief, how can you want a woman who is so much less beautiful than you? Everything is still a question.

Promise me that you are not leaving your intended solely because of me. It must be because it is right for you and you alone. I need more time with you, by letter or face to face, to know if we are right for each other. You have asked for my heart, and I am inclined to believe I can give it. But please do not ask for my hand until we are both sure of it.

With deep affection,
Emma

A letter arrived almost every day now, from Lillian or Sev and sometimes from Timothy who found a way to tease a smile from Emma.

...How could you, my dear Emma? I am bewitched by this woman that you paired me with to run your boarding house. I love her completely. But Emma, her family!

The mother fawns over me which I can understand as I am such a lovable gentleman. However, I sneeze and blubber whenever the little beast she calls Muffin is anywhere near me. Would she notice if I replaced this cat with a ferret?

And little brother Alfred! Save me from this adolescent boy. He steadfastly refuses to take orders from me, telling me I am not his brother or father (God forbid). Yet he trails behind me, cow-eyed for a man's time and attention. Do you realize nobody has so much as taught the lad to saw a board? Worse yet, how to strike a sliotar with his hurley, even though the lovely Gaelic sport is to be an Olympic event this year. An outrage! In your bag of medical tricks, do you have any tonics to help rush a boy into manhood?

It is much to ask that the mother and brother come along with the lady I love, my girl. You set your friend Timothy quite a task.

Emma laughed as she finished his letter but realized his complaint rang true. She, too, found Alfred a difficult youngster. Timothy could have his hands full there. But then again, so might Alfred. In her next letter to Lillian, she addressed the subject. Lillian was quick to reply.

...I love my little brother but must admit he can be a ninnyhammer. He was only eight when our father died, and he found it hard that a big sister assumed the head of the family station. I understand he could be worried that Timothy will take me away from the family. But Alfred is so hostile, he even called Timothy a bog-trotter the other day. I'm sure Alfred has no idea what it means (actually, neither do I), just that it is inappropriate for an Irishman. The lad was punished with a day in his room. It will be a week the next time.

Emma had no tested wisdom with adolescent boys, but she was a woman of strong opinions, nonetheless.

... Lillian, I know how it feels to lose a father, too. It makes sense to me that Alfred lost one man and may well not want to take a chance of losing another. Accepting Timothy is daunting for the boy since he no doubt thinks of himself as the head of the family. Given time, Timothy will win him over, as he appears to

do with one and all. Alfred will realize that caring for you and your mother is a weight Timothy can lift off his young shoulders. Time will cure this issue, time and patience from Timothy and you.

In March the days grew drier, longer, and warmer, causing early spring plants to raise their heads at last. Emma became increasingly excited about the harvest to come. She hoped Willa would appear soon so they could search the woods and meadows together. In the meantime, she took a long walk out the narrow strip of land called Ediz Hook, toward the lighthouse at its end. Natives lived all along the spit, and another white woman might not make the hike. But another woman was not Emma, who had distaste for ignorance about the tribes. Besides, another woman did not own a great burly dog like Koira.

To the north, the Strait was calm, with gray clouds allowing occasional bursts of sun. A constant breeze smelled of salt and seaweed. Emma could see across the twenty-five miles to Vancouver Island, picking out the Victoria settlement on the coast. Sidney, Severin's home, was out of her sight, far to the Northeast. A disturbance in the water drew her eyes closer to the Hook where a humpback whale breeched, noisily blowing water into the air.

The shipwrecked *Clallam* was somewhere out there, too, sixty-five fathoms down. Two bodies had been found floating off this very Hook, two weeks after the shipwreck. It brought the harrowing event back to Emma; she spotted then lost a dark lump in the water. Body or seal? Emma vowed to Koira, "I'll not sail this Strait again if I have anything to say about it."

Severin had been right to believe the US would be more lenient than Canada. The newspapers reported that the official US Marine Inspection Board revoked the chief engineer's license and suspended the captain's license for one year. In Canada, a coroner's jury declared Captain Roberts guilty of manslaughter by virtue of gross negligence. The captain went into seclusion in his Seattle home, and that was that.

Turning to head back along the Hook, Emma faced the protected harbor to the south. She stared at Port Angeles, grey and rugged, clinging to the waterfront like a limpet. Behind it, the snowy Olympics rose above forested hills. A landslide could flush the little town into the harbor at anytime. A flooded creek had leveled part of it once. It was rebuilt. Then a fire burned it to the ground. Still, it was rebuilt. The mountains shimmered in sun before clouds closed again. Emma had no doubt they were daring her to think any part of this wilderness was under control. Land here could be as dangerous as water.

Koira had been swimming in the harbor, his webbed feet and rudder-like tail carrying him quickly to a floating log to flush off the sunning cormorants. Paddling back to the beach, he shook himself and came to Emma where she sat on a dry log. His wide grin sent drool droplets into the wind. Emma stroked his wet head. The Newfie was her closest confidante. "I have a confession, Koira."

His ears reacted to the sound of his name.

"I have missed my time of the month not once but twice. What on earth will I do about this situation?"

Koira knew humans often babbled sounds even the wisest of dogs did not understand. This struck him as one of those times. He tore down the pebbled beach to grab a long piece of kelp in case Emma wanted to give it a toss in the air. It always made him feel better so it might work for her, too.

* * *

The next day, Emma found swampy patches along the dirt road to Sequim. Skunk cabbage was bursting out of the wet ground. It was far too early to harvest the roots, but she enjoyed their bright yellow blooms. They looked like elf-sized lanterns to her. On a hill above them, out of the damp, she discovered a second sign of spring. Wild violets would make a lovely aromatic tea to fight Birdie's asthma and give her a break from the bitter hickory brew.

Emma invited Molly to the Axton kitchen, using the sampling of violet tea as an excuse. She did not want to talk in front of Otis. Confessing she'd lied to them would be easier to one than to both. She was glad Betty Axton was at the hardware store picking up a new faucet Axe had ordered.

"I told you I have a fiancé," Emma said to Molly, after taking a sip of tea for courage.

"Oh, Emma," Molly enthused. "I've wanted to ask all about him, but when you didn't mention him anymore, I thought maybe he had broken the engagement and broken your heart, as well, and it was all so painful that you never wanted to mention him again."

Emma nearly laughed. If she'd thought up that story herself, she might have used it. But the whole point was to tell Molly the truth.

"No. I lied to you, Molly. I do not have a fiancé at all."

Molly's hand stopped short with a cookie on its way to her mouth. "But why would you say you did if you didn't?"

"Oh Molly, I panicked! I was so afraid you wouldn't believe I wasn't here for Otis. I felt on the spot, and a lie simply tumbled out. When we became such friends, I didn't want to tell you I'd lied to you. I am so sorry."

Molly's lower lip trembled, whether with disapproval or anger or hurt, Emma didn't know. "Please speak to me,

Molly. I would never do such a thing now that we are so close." Emma reached for Molly's non-cookie hand.

Molly relented. "Well, yes, I can see how that might have happened. I did act rather badly that day we met. And, frankly, the truth that you are available will tickle Otis. Every single man in town has asked him about you, and he is tired of holding them at bay."

"What?" Now it was Emma's turn to gape.

"Yes, silly goose. How many single women of means do you suppose the men of Port Angeles have a chance to meet?"

"Well, tell Otis to just keep turning them away. Besides, I have something else I must tell you. I am pregnant."

"Pregnant!"

"Yes. The father is the man who is not my fiancé."

"Who is this man? Don't tell me he attacked you." Molly's eyes widened and her hands flew to her cheeks.

Molly lived on the edge of fantasy, her imagination often out of control. Sometimes it delighted Emma, and other times it felt like she needed to pull the reins rather sharply. Times like now. So she confessed with a blush. "Not at all. If anything, I attacked him. I am a scarlet woman."

Molly huffed. "Well, maybe in Seattle. But out here? It takes more than a baby to fall from grace. You need not join the girls at Angel's Parlor just yet."

"So you do not think less of me?"

Molly beamed. "Fimble-famble! Oh, Emma, we have so much to plan! It will give me practice for when Otis and I are with child. Now then. What name will you choose? I love the name Jessica for a girl, don't you?" Molly was off and running. "But what fun to tailor a tiny suit for a baby boy..."

Betty Axton interrupted when she came in the backdoor with Axe's faucet and the mail. "Hello, Molly. Another letter for you, Emma. So much mail! I feel downright unpopular."

"Please join us, Betty, and try the violet tea. It will be good for Birdie. And I have news you should hear as well." Emma told Betty her story. Hopefully her landlady would not toss her out for egregious conduct.

Apparently not. But Betty was far more practical than Molly, aware of the fix Emma was in. "It will be hard, raising a child on this frontier with no husband to help. Is it possible the father can be reached?" Betty looked pointedly at the letter from Severin Eronen.

Emma shrugged. The problem wasn't whether he could be reached but should he be reached. While Betty and Molly discussed the arrival of a baby, Emma quickly read her letter.

Darling Emma,

I write this the same day I heard from you. I go to sea again this afternoon, so I have only a moment and will write more soon. Jorin and I are holding strong. My parents don't understand why I choose to work the ocean instead of the forest, but they know they are losing the battle. And they would rather have this Finnish girl for Jorin than lose her all together. I will soon be out of this commitment. Oh, and to answer your question, her name is Helleena.

No, it is not because of you that I want to be free. It is because, having met you, I realize what I am missing if I do NOT take such action. Whether you will have me or not, I will be better off without a woman and way of life that I will never love.

So there you have it. I am my own man in this. I find you not guilty of any actions I take. That said, can we now move past this and contemplate the possibility of a future together? Trust me when I say I can be a very stubborn fellow.

Yours,

Sev

Maybe Sev could be a very stubborn fellow. But how would he handle knowing he was to be a father? What if he came for her? What if he didn't?

CHAPTER FOURTEEN

Port Angeles, Strait of Juan de Fuca
April, 1904

Emma hadn't realized how much a person could vomit. Morning sickness kept her leashed to the privies at the Axton home and her office. Owning a spittoon had never crossed her mind before, but one now hid under her desk in case she was overcome while working with a patient. She began to think the baby wasn't a child of Sev but of Satan. Emma tried her own remedies for waves of nausea plus those from the pharmacy, but it made little difference. Dr. Obermayer might have a secret tonic, but she'd rather vomit than go see him. So she waited it out, and in a matter of weeks, it stopped. The aroma of bacon frying or mint sauce or floral shampoo no longer distressed her, and she could hold down something other than Uneeda Biscuits. The Axtons and the Combes were both clearly delighted when Emma returned to a pleasant frame of mind.

In the afternoons, she continued to add patients. A frantic farm woman stopped with three children, all with pinworms. After providing a tincture of mugwart to use orally, and to apply around their anuses to relieve the itch, Emma told all the kids to quit sucking their thumbs and wash their hands after they scratched their bottoms. She told their mother to cut their fingernails short. And the poor woman had no idea she needed to wash herself, as well, after handling their underwear. It surprised Emma how often basic hygiene was a mystery to her patients.

Awa, the bouncer from Angel's Parlor, stopped by, thrilling Molly with his exotic appearance. He brought a bouquet of fresh-picked avalanche lilies from the Angels for Emma, and he requested help with a wound he'd tried to stitch himself. Emma snapped at him for such nonsense while she wrapped his arm in an oversized yarrow poultice. Awa was as contrite as a colossus could muster.

The patient who worried Emma the most was a young woman who lived two residences from the Axton house. She suffered severe menstrual pain. Dr. Obermayer gave her a solution that curbed it, but it made her listless, nauseous. Emma sniffed the bottle and frowned in suspicion. Too many women were dispensed legal concoctions containing opiates or cocaine for female problems.

Emma felt called upon for the greatest of diplomacy regarding this lady who was not much younger than she herself. "Dr. Obermayer is a fine doctor, Miss Harding, but he is not a woman. So let's talk woman to woman.

"I prefer you attempt more feminine remedies for your cramps and pain. It may take time, because every woman is different, but there are many solutions to try. You will have menses for a long time to come, so you want to discover what works best for you.

"The women I know with issues like yours all take Chamomile tea, lots of it, during their times of the month. Sprinkle cinnamon on your food, especially if you suffer nausea. Seek black cohosh at the pharmacy. Between those three undertakings, you will likely experience relief.

"Now, this is important. When pain strikes, rest on your back with a hot water bottle over your uterus until the heat is expended. Then massage your abdomen for a few minutes." She had the woman lie on her exam table while she demonstrated the area in question and the way to rub. "Your body will relax and the pain should release its clutches. In upcoming months there are other things we can try. Do not give up hope."

When the woman left, Emma sighed. She could see that a conflict with Dr. Obermayer was unavoidable. She was sure as eggs is eggs of that.

One warm April afternoon, Emma found a letter from Sev awaiting her in her room. She surprised herself how joyous she felt, since she hadn't heard in so long. Joy presented itself as tears. "What on earth?" she blubbered to Koira. "I had no idea how I missed hearing from him! Or is the baby plucking my heartstrings?" The envelope looked frayed and dirty as she stared at the postmark. It had been at sea for many days before finding its way back from the wilds of Canada.

Dearest Emma,

Now I have time to write, but will not have opportunity to mail this missive for some while. It is night off the west coast of Vancouver Island. A calm sea, following winds. The lantern swings over my head with enough light to compose, our vessel gently rocks, and it is quiet in the crew quarters this late.

I am on a large old ferry bound for northern Alaskan ports with a stop on the way in Dawson City. That wild settlement is smaller than it was a few years back when Klondikers lost their shirts while seeking gold, but it still exists. I can mail letters from there, with some assurance they will arrive at your door.

I hated to leave you so far away, but all the hours that I crew these steamers, I build my reputation as a dependable seaman. I hope to be an engineer one day...possibly a captain? Ah, such plans! I intend to be a man of means for the lady who has turned my head.

In your last letter you asked questions I did not have time to answer, but I can do them justice now.

What are your hobbies, you asked. I can, as part of my profession, repair steam engines. I built a very small one of scrap copper in a wooden boat that my sister's boy sails on a pond. I guess that makes me a toymaker.

As a little boy I had a lengthy illness, and my mother taught me how to knit to pass the hours. She often spun yarn from cattail fluff and dog hair; the old Salish woman who worked for us showed her how. I will make a sweater from dog hair yarn for Koira as he may recognize one of his own. He will love me the more for it, although I hope I do not receive a dose of fleas! Normally I use regular sheep wool yarn, of course. I am teased by my shipmates while I knit, until they see how warm my scarves, hats, and sweaters keep me.

I love to read and to sing although I am told I do not do the latter well. I brew fairly good beer but am a disastrous cook. My newest and favorite hobby is to think about you.

You asked how I feel about the vote for women. Women work for their country so they should vote for it. What other viewpoint is there? As to my religious beliefs, like nearly all Finns, I was Lutheran by birth. But the spirits who guide me now are not constrained to any box church I know.

How can I want a woman who is less beautiful than me? What a question! Are you teasing me, looking for a compliment? Do you not know you are a beauty? I see the intelligence dance in your pale eyes. Your spectacles only enhance it. Nobody appears smarter than my Emma, although you are tempered with sadness. You have experienced enough to give your intelligence meaning. Yet freckles play across your nose to keep you from becoming too serious. You are a muddle of joy and sorrow so I must keep my eyes on you at all times, like a sailor watching changes in the clouds and the stars.

Emma, I have held your narrow waist against me, felt your
softness on my chest, filled my hand with the spread of your hips.
You fit me perfectly. There is more beauty in that than in all the
dancehall girls on the coast. Your husband was insane to let you
escape.
    God willing, that escape will lead to a capture by
    Your own true servant,
    Sev

Emma cried for an hour after reading her love letter.
Great drippy hiccups, gasps, and snorts. It must be the baby
in her belly causing such turmoil, or so she said to Betty
Axton who heard her bawling in her room and asked if she
was well.

Emma had to do something about this situation. To
herself alone, she admitted she was afraid. His words were
a balm for her insecurities, as much as her potions were for
her patients' wounds. Yet she feared Severin might
disappear if he knew about the child.

She didn't want to confess, but he had to know. It was
time. It would take forever for a letter to find him, and she
must write it.

Dear Sev,
Whether this letter is a goodbye or not will be up to you. I
have something I must share that could determine our fate.
    You are going to be a father. As of this writing, I am three
months with child. If this is the result of one night in a loft, what
do you suppose would happen after another two or three?
    Not a time to tease, I suppose. I have known about this for
some weeks, but it is fresh for you. I hope you find my news blissful
for you, as it is for me.
    Darling Sev, I am a strong, independent woman. I could raise
this baby on my own. I don't worry about society's disapproval.

*If you choose not to have a relationship with your child and me,
we will survive. But I confess, I hope that is not your decision. I
want you to be a part of our life. You occupy space in my heart
that will only grow if I factor into your plans.*

*As I said at the beginning of this letter, a goodbye is up to
you. But know that your Emma is terrified of hearing you use the
word.*

Write soon, dear one,

Emma

* * *

One day in late April, when Emma and Koira arrived
at their office, Willa was waiting out front. Her Klallam
family had hiked miles inland to the hot springs for a
traditional cleansing of spirit. The pools there could reach
over one hundred degrees and had been used by tribes for
centuries. After their gathering, Willa left them to trek down
the trail to Port Angeles.

Emma hugged her, and Koira, ridiculous beast, nearly
knocked her down with enthusiastic paws to her shoulders.
Emma ushered her inside to meet Molly and to see her new
office. Then the two closed up shop and headed into the
wilds.

"He is your protector in the wilderness?" Willa asked.

"I have no idea," Emma answered. "I presume he'd lick
someone to distraction. Death by slobber."

For three days, they walked the waterfront, riverside,
and woodland trails as Emma harvested medicinal
seaweed, mosses, bark, and flowers. In the evenings, they
created tinctures, teas, elixirs, and salves and hung drying
plants from every curtain rod and peg. The women warmed
concoctions on the small wood stove in the office,
generating enough heat for Willa to stay there overnight,
using the exam table as a bed. Emma provided many

medicines new to Willa in payment for the Klallam native's knowledge. Willa promised to return in the summer when she could and definitely in September, in time to birth Emma's baby. She was experienced in such things and would teach Molly to help. Willa's calm assurance next to Molly's overwrought enthusiasm put Emma at ease. "Molly and Koira are a lot alike," Willa observed.

On the fourth day, she was gone. There was no sign of her in Emma's office, other than the drying plants and shelves now filled with bottle and tins. To Emma, her office at last had a curative aroma of fresh botanicals, as if the very air could soothe an infection, calm an emotion, relieve a pain.

Feeling lonely, Emma went to the reception area to sit with Molly. Otis received the *Seattle Daily Times*, several issues arriving together about a week after their publication dates. Emma and Molly enjoyed the papers when no patients awaited either practitioner. Emma missed trips to the Bon Marché or to Wallin & Nordstrom for shoes. Molly desperately wanted to visit the city's brand new McCarthy dry goods store. The two friends consulted the ads together.

"Twelve dollar men's suits! I could make one for ten."

"Gadzooks! Look at these white slippers with the bows on their toes. And the narrow straps on these."

"Imagine the fabrics! Hundreds, they say."

"Can you see a dress like this surviving one day on these streets?"

"Not on a lady with hips like mine. I have a built-in bustle." Molly was aware of her amplitude.

Emma missed vaudeville at the Crystal Theatre, musical comedy at the Grand Opera, and the Seattle Symphony at Christensen Hall. Could she go back for just a few days to see the boarding house, the theatre, the new stores? No, probably not. Cutter might yet appear, although

Emma thought he had taken on a sort of boogeyman status to her, a scary nightmare that was no longer real.

An article caught Emma's eye. It was the first mention she'd seen regarding a world fair planned to open in Portland in just over a year.

"Such a thing in Oregon. Can you imagine that, Molly? They're calling it the Lewis and Clark Centennial and American Pacific Exposition and Oriental Fair."

"I can imagine a fair but not who would name it that."

"They say countries around the world will send exhibits. Everything modern. Wouldn't you love to see something like that?"

"Not I. A tailor convention, maybe. But not a collection of machines and ideas far beyond my ken."

Emma thought it would be wonderful. The whole world just a year and a railroad trip away. And it wasn't in Seattle. It was in Portland. A boogeyman would never find her there.

CHAPTER FIFTEEN

Port Angeles, Strait of Juan de Fuca
April, 1904

The days passed, life on the frontier bursting with spring promise. For Emma, each day was busy with treating patients, harvesting medicinal plants, sewing baby clothes, and longing for a letter from Severin.

For Koira, a new worry was added to his list of responsibilities.

School would soon be out for the summer. Meanwhile, Birdie walked home along a dirt road, sometimes cutting through the woods. The little girl's breathing had improved enough that Emma dared think she might outgrow her asthma. Her episodes happened less often with less discomfort. Birdie missed fewer days of class and enjoyed playing outdoors with Koira.

The big dog varied his routine for the little girl. Before joining Emma at her office in the morning, he began walking Birdie to school, ears cocked as she babbled an eight-year-old's secrets to him. In the afternoon, he met her to walk her home. His new self-appointed role delighted Betty. "I know Birdie cuts through the woods, even though I tell her not to," she said to Emma. "Her teacher told me Koira arrives just as she releases the children at the end of the school day. The others can be cruel about Birdie's spells, but Koira gives them something to envy. He minds her commands and totally ignores theirs."

At the evening meal, Birdie was filled with stories of "Big Puppy did this" or "Big Puppy did that" as she recapped her day. Therefore, it was a great surprise when the child burst in the door one afternoon, dirty and upset, followed by a crestfallen Newfie. Emma and Betty, each sewing at the kitchen table where the light was best, tried to calm the troubled child so they could understand her story.

"I'm all dirty. My dress is torn," Birdie cried. "Koira did it."

"Slow down, Birdie...Koira did it?...Take a breath...What happened?" Emma and Betty clucked in unison.

"Koira jumped on me and knocked me down."

"He did what?" The two women were a duet of disbelief. Emma looked at the accused only to receive a sheepish dog smile in return.

"I was playing with the kitties. They're so cute. One even purred."

The women cast a glance at each other and shrugged. Betty turned back to Birdie and asked, "What kitties?"

"Koira didn't like it. He wouldn't stop whining. I told him to be quiet, but he wouldn't."

"Whose kitties? Where were they?" Emma tried for an answer.

"I heard them meow and found them under a log in the woods." Birdie huffed, sounding short-tempered with these two slow-witted adults. Then she must have realized what she'd revealed and instantly turned contrite. "I know I shouldn't have been there, Momma."

"No. You shouldn't. But what happened?"

"That's when I saw the momma cat. She was running at us kinda screaming. Koira growled at her, then grabbed my dress and pulled me away from the kittens. He tore it, see?" She indicted a ragged hem. "That big kitty stopped to see if her babies were okay. Koira kept pulling on me."

"Oh my God." Betty's face paled. She dropped to her knees to hug her child.

"When she roared at us, I got scared," Birdie confessed. "I couldn't move."

"Are you hurt?" Emma tried to find cat scratches. Claws could infect...claws could kill. She saw none, but her heart raced.

"She came at me. Then I could move. I ran and ran. Koira was behind me. I coughed so much I couldn't breathe, so I had to stop." Birdie's tears ran rivulets of mud down her dirty face. "Koira knocked me down. He laid on top of me. I got all dirty. I'm sorry, Momma."

Betty was so ashen that Emma feared she might faint. But she clung to her child, cooing, "It's all over. You're safe, my sweet."

"Koira kept growling at that cat. He sounded so mean, and he drooled on my head. I looked out under his chin. That cat crouched. Koira didn't move, and neither did she. He growled, and she hissed. Finally, she gave up and left."

"Oh, Birdie! How brave you were." Betty was crying now, too. "Koira, what a good dog."

"I told him to get off, but he didn't. Not 'til the kitties followed their momma out of sight. I hope she's not too mad at them. I hope you're not too mad at me."

Betty gave Birdie's shoulders a squeeze and demanded, "Promise me you'll stay away from those kittens if you see them again. Promise."

"I promise. Don't be mad at Koira, Miss Emma. He didn't mean to get me dirty. I was mad then, but I know he helped me."

"I think you both were very brave," said Emma.

At dinner that evening, Betty told Axe he might want to look for cougar tracks on the trail to the school. And Koira was given an elk bone that still had a lovely bit of meat.

April 14
Dear Emma,

A baby! Conceived on an island following a shipwreck. How very romantic...thank you for sharing this love story with me. I am delighted for you, as you sound so happy for yourself. And, of course, we don't expect you to be here for the wedding, not unless we hear that Cutter is at the bottom of the sea, or otherwise dead and gone forever.

I'll share your news with Timothy, but not with my mother. I am sure you understand that she is a woman of traditional values. I chuckle at the idea of you showing up here to be my bridesmaid, your belly coming down the aisle before you do. Mother might succumb to a case of the vapors! Shame on me for laughing at her in this way.

All is well on this side of Puget Sound. Timothy is teaching Alfred some crazy Irish sport, and he tells me that Alfred asked him about girls. He would say no more about it. I believe the two are keeping secrets from me.

Mother's cat Muffin has disappeared. Maybe he took on a mouse that turned out to be more like a rat. Timothy instantly replaced the cat with a puppy for Mother. It is an adorable little thing, although yappy, and has turned her head. She calls it Fluffy. Interestingly, Timothy does not sneeze around dogs. Hmmmm. Do you find anything suspicious in this story?

The Braxton suffragettes, myself included, are planning a march this summer. We are so close to winning the right to vote; I hold out hope that Washington will be the first state in this century to allow such a thing. What a day that will be. Of course, Timothy grumbles that maybe women should be allowed to vote, but my mother should not be allowed to name an animal!

Now, back to the baby. Have you told your Canadian? Don't be silly about this, Emma. I know you will think he won't want to be tied to you. You do not value yourself as others do. Please remember, that blighter Ronan is not the model for good men. Besides, the baby is Severin's as well as yours. Whether the two of you form a couple or not, the baby deserves to love you both.

If you have told him, what is his reply? Write soon to your loving

Lillian

P.S. The damn cat just came home. Now we have two animals who despise each other, and frankly, I am fond of neither.

April 26

Dearest Lillian,

My belly begins to protrude but I'm afraid I couldn't embarrass your mother very much quite yet. However it is best that I do not try! You make me giggle, and I appreciated it more than you can know. Thank you for being a good enough friend to understand I don't need marriage to raise a child.

Yes, I have written to Sev. I await his reply now. He is on a ship somewhere in the north country so I assume my letters may not reach him until he returns to his home.

I long not merely to hear from him but actually to see him. Only to you do I admit I'm terrified of his rejection. If that happens, I will go on, of course. You always go on. But happiness seems so close that I wish I could reach out and grab it. Sorrow for my mother, fear of Cutter, loss of my life the way it was...none of those things matter quite so much when Sev is near. I sound a great deal like a bawling calf even to my own ears.

Molly has planned a party for two days hence, in the lobby of the only hotel in Port Angeles. It is to introduce our three businesses...her husband's dentistry, my eclectic medical office, and her own tailoring trade to the community at large. She has made a handsome suit for Axe to wear and one for Otis. Both men

are well turned out models, so people will see what she can do. She
asked to make one for Dr. Obermayer, but he turned her down.
What a sourpuss that man is. I will write more about the event
after it happens.

When she is not so busy, I will ask Molly to make me a dress
with ample breast and belly room although she does not like to sew
clothing for women. I'll inform her a large sack will do!

In closing, I know now what to get as a wedding gift for you
and Timothy. A matched set of bunny rabbits, I think, to hop
around the house with the dog and cat.

With love,

Emma

Emma was in her office. Between patients, she was standing on a chair to dust the top shelves. With no warning, Dr. Obermayer burst through her door with Molly skittering after him, ordering him to stop. The door slammed against the wall with such force, Emma's framed Eclectic Physician License shimmied to a tilt.

"It's all right, Molly." Emma hoped her voice didn't tremble or her knees knock. She stepped down from the chair and faced the furious man. She tried to arrange her countenance in as stern a look as his. He glared, and Emma knew why. She thought "*Miss Harding*" as the doctor snapped, "Miss Harding. She tells me you disrespected me, told her to forget the medicine I provide to her."

"I..."

"How dare you turn a patient against me. A common bit of gullyfluff like you. I will have this charlatan business of yours shut down immediately."

It was a race; her anger and her fear were in a dead heat. *Imagine the arrogance of this man!* Emma channeled her mother and hissed, "Dr. Obermayer, you will do no such thing. And please keep your voice down in my office. If you believe you have lost a patient, then you need to question yourself, not me."

"I'll spread the word so fast around this town, you'll be ruined."

Emma took a seat at her desk, lest she fall. "My good sir, this town has worse to hear about you than about me."

For a second he paused, lifting his eyebrows as if confused. "What are you flapping your yap about?" He slapped his fist on her desk. "You dare question an actual doctor?"

"I question any actual doctor who gives a healthy young woman a bottle of opium. There is not an informed physician left in the nation who still believes such nonsense is ethical or called for. It's soon to be illegal according to most educated sources, should you choose to read any. Yet you continue to drug heaven knows how many women and men."

"I will listen to no more of this hogwash."

Emma stood again, feeling steady now that she was on the attack. Later, she would realize that letting loose was rather fun. She leaned over her desk and pointed at him. "You will listen. I will let it be known you are creating addicts out of innocent people. I suspect you've even created one out of yourself, the way you are so often out of control."

She thought he would slap her. He pulled back his hand but Koira's growl caused him to lower it again. Until that second, the dog's presence must have gone unnoticed by the doctor. Now Emma growled as well. "Do not threaten me again, and I will keep my counsel. Leave my office and do not return. You do your job, and I will do mine."

The physician threw open the office door which slammed against the wall again, causing Emma's license to dance a jig once more. Molly yelped at the noise, and Otis emerged from the dental office just long enough to see the irate doctor stalk out the front door, not bothering to shut it as he stormed away.

Silence descended. Emma slumped back in her chair, shaken and fighting back tears, but feeling a secret burst of pride. Weakly she said, "Thank you for doing your job, too, Koira."

Molly appeared in her doorway. She looked ready to burst into giggles. "Gosh, Emma. I take it the good doctor was a difficult patient this morning."

Relief shot through Emma, and she laughed. Molly let loose, too, and they giggled like schoolgirls, at least until a male voice behind her startled them both into silence. "I will try to be an altogether better patient than the man who just bolted past me on the street."

Molly turned. Emma stood. Koira barked. And Severin strolled into the office.

* * *

Emma could not stop her tears. She was pregnant, she'd been yelled at like never before, her mother had paid a visit from beyond, and her lover had returned. All she got out was, "Oh," as she crossed the office toward Severin. Koira got there first, nearly beating the crewman to death with his tail.

"Out of the way, you great hairy beast," Severin said, pushing past the Newfie. He folded Emma to him. "Ah, I've missed this. And both of my arms work now to hold you doubly close."

"Oh," she managed again before they kissed.

He leaned back to say, "Let me look at you. By god, you are even more beautiful that I remember. Possibly it is the rose in your cheeks from such a tongue lashing you gave that man."

"Ahem," said Molly. "I'll just go now." She shut the door but Emma paid her no mind.

Another kiss, this time sustained with sweetness and longing.

Finally, Emma found her voice. "How did you get here?"

"By sea, of course. Ferry dropped me off, then went on its way."

"But, Sev, did you get my letter? About the..."

"About our baby? Yes, it was forwarded from home on another vessel to Sitka, and I received it there. I made it here as fast as I could." He cupped her chin in his hand. "Yes, Emma, I want you. I want you and our baby. I'm here to stake my claim as surely as one of the miners I've met."

She grinned. "You're positive you're not suffering Klondike fever?"

He groaned. "Maybe you should refrain from jokes lest our baby overhear and take up vaudeville."

"Or maybe you're dazzled by fool's gold?"

"I've never known anything so real in my life as the way I feel about you."

                           * * *

Two days later, the party for the three new practitioners was held in the hotel lobby. Most of the little settlement came, except the town doctor. Some may have been disappointed that there was no liquor in the punch, but Betty, Molly, and Emma made sure plates were full. And the Sequim fiddler who entertained was surprisingly good. Otis booked two new dental appointments, Miss Harding introduced Emma to several of her friends, and the undertaker commissioned a suit from Molly so the event was deemed a business success.

A last-minute entertainment was added to the occasion. A Methodist clergyman, the circuit rider for outlying towns on the Peninsula, pronounced Severin Eronen and Emma Prescott husband and wife.

May 2

Dearest Lillian,

What a whirlwind. Where to begin?

Well, I suppose I start by telling you that from now on, you address your letters to Mrs. Severin Eronen. Yes, that is correct. I have married a second time before you have managed your first. There is something to be said for not having a mother involved to make complex arrangements (although I wish she and Gran could know Sev and how wonderful he is)!

He simply arrived one day in the flesh, with his plans complete. He told his employers he will continue to crew their vessels, but now based in the US instead of Canada. He can transfer on the mosquito fleet to any port where he is needed.

He settled all complications at home, or at least his brother Jorin did. While Sev was on the way to Alaska, the intended bride, Helleena, arrived in Victoria. Jorin met her there, and they soon were inseparable. Sev's parents finally accept that the wedding they plan will be for their younger son. In the meantime, their older boy 'eloped.' I suppose I will meet his family one day and must be prepared for their disapproval. Unless of course, their grandbaby wins the day for me.

Severin arrived here ready to marry, and I could not think of a single reason why we shouldn't. He is so pleased about fatherhood he has begun to knit baby clothes. What a lucky woman I am!

I will stay at the Axton home, at least until the baby is born. Sev will be at sea more weeks than in Port Angeles, but he promises to be here in September when the baby is due. My dear Lillian, I think this is a fine solution for us both, to have our individual lives as they were, but also our new lives as husband and wife, father and mother. I only wish he craved a life on land instead of the water. I understand all too well why the ocean is called the widow-maker, and that I could not abide.

But enough of that worry. My life, quite astoundingly, overwhelms me at the moment with how little I have to fret about! Only the occasional nightmare of Cutter darkens my mood.

I have at last decided on a wedding gift, not just for you and Timothy, but for Sev and me, as well. I made the purchase with the last of the gold given to me by Harry Tracy; it is fit I share it with others. I've acquired all necessary tickets for the four of us to attend the Lewis and Clark Centennial Exposition in Portland, Oregon next spring. I truly believe this is the event of the new century...something we will tell our grandchildren about when we are all in our fifties, rocking on the porch of an old folks home. Details will follow.

Your loving friend,
Emma

Emma, my girl,

If that Canadian Finn of yours does anything to harm you, call on your old hooligan. I looked after you once and will do so again. He's a lucky man, and he better remember that.

Timothy

Dearest Emma,

As your time grows near I think of you often. How rotund you must be now...can you reach around your belly to listen to your patients' hearts? Can you bend to pick a flower without tipping over? Do you have cravings for oddities? In case it helps, I have enclosed my mother's recipe for watermelon pickles.

How flabbergasted little Birdie must be by the whole process, although from your description, she might well be more help than Molly. Here is an important duty to assign the child; give Birdie

*the enclosed postcard, have her mark "It's a Boy" or "It's a Girl,"
and mail it to me the very second she knows.*

*Now then. About the baby name. I understand you do not
wish to use Timothy or Lillian as I suggested, although we truly
don't intend a baby of our own. Timothy appears to have inherited
my little brother to father. They are now recommending books to
each other. Both loved* Treasure Island, *Alfred now fantasizes
about being a pirate, and maybe Timothy does, too. He threatens
to share* Fanny Hill *with Alfred, but I warned him against
sharing those passages with anyone but me.*

*Your baby girl could be another Emma or Minerva, of course.
I don't believe I ever knew your Gran's name. Your middle name
would be another generation honoring Susan B. Anthony. A boy
could be Sev or Jorin or William; the latter was your father's
name, was it not? Well, I suppose Betty and Molly and I should
hold our peace and allow the two of you to choose the perfect name
on your own. But I do so love to give advice!*

*We have another new boarder so we are now a full house. The
lady is a widow, one who writes poetry that she demands to recite
aloud. We are all finding we have other obligations that keep us
out of the parlor in the evenings. This may not have been my best
of selections for the Prescott Boarding House.*

*Mother is making me two new dresses for the Lewis and
Clark Exposition. It is still months away but I am so excited. Did
you know that it coincides with the National American Woman
Suffrage Association convention? It happens from June 29 until
July 4 so we will be in Portland. We must spend time with the
suffrage leaders while Timothy and Sev visit the machinery
exhibits.*

*Can you imagine us all actually observing a flying blimp and
a motion picture? Or traveling the Orient through a palace and
seeing the Carnival of Venice? Oh, my dear friend, I am*

All keyed up!

Lillian

Over the summer, Severin made the case that Emma should travel to Port Townsend to be near a doctor in the autumn.

"I am a doctor," she pouted.

"Yes, but you will be otherwise occupied."

"That's why Willa is to be here. She will be my hands. We know what to do. Molly, who I admit knows nothing, will assist. Thankfully, Betty Axton will be just down the hall."

"But..."

"But we are all women, so how could we possibly handle this situation which is as old as human time?" Emma narrowed her gaze.

Severin knew when it was better to walk away from the very-round, very opinionated pregnant lady he loved. Koira knew, too. The two of them bonded on many walks around town together.

As promised, Willa appeared in early September. She spent nights in Emma's office as she had before, although Emma no longer made the walk from the Axton house each day. Willa was so helpful she even provided Awa with the fungal cream required by one of the Angels and replenished Birdie's violet tea supply.

Severin knew Emma's room at the Axton house would soon be too small. He kept watch for a family-sized home.

"I'm family-sized now," said Emma, grumpy with her girth. She could no longer sleep anywhere but in a rocker and could no longer squat on a chamber pot. Lack of sleep and countless trips to the privy were both deadly to her moods.

"Our child may not be ready to meet us, but I am more than ready for it," she moaned, stretching her back.

All was in place and ready by September, except for Severin whose ferry broke down off Neah Bay. Willa handled this part of the birth, too. In some mysterious way that Emma never quite understood, Willa got word of the disabled vessel from the Makah tribe on the Washington coast. She sent a message back to them. A Makah canoe approached the anchored ferry, and the assistant engineer was requested. Severin was lowered by rope into their dugout, and the powerful oarsmen rowed him to Port Angeles. He never doubted Willa again.

Emma went into labor nine months from the night in the Smith Island barn (she and Sev now referred to that sheep loft as their Pleasure Dome, although both were pleased by a real bed). The birth was as painful and messy as she expected, but over much sooner. The baby girl slipped into Willa's arms, and onto Emma's breast as faultlessly as a well-executed military exercise. Everyone did their jobs to perfection, including Molly who provided an endless parade of clean towels and encouraging words.

In honor of the first poultice given by Willa to Emma months ago, and for the tea that soothed Birdie's cough, the baby girl was named Violet.

Dear Lillian,

I assume Birdie's postcard arrived bearing the news that Severin and I have a baby girl named Violet. She shows all the signs of being another in the line of independent-minded Prescott women. Her schedule of events in no way takes ours into account. While I am in a merry mood again, Violet makes up for it by issuing her opinion loudly and clearly when I am not speedy enough with the diaper or the breast.

Sev looks at Violet as a great miracle of his own creation, and she is pleased to be treated as one. She has stolen his heart. Only Koira remains faithful to me, and his attention can easily be drawn away by Birdie. Oh, the inconsistency of men!

Sev will soon go to sea again, leaving his womenfolk behind. Do not be surprised if he appears at your door one day in that Seattle is frequently a stopping point, but not usually long enough for him to leave the ferry. He is anxious to meet my good friends.

I will miss him, of course, but will be glad to get back to my office. Violet will go with me; Molly is eager for her company. I have not asked Otis his opinion on a baby in the office, but Molly and I together are a formidable obstacle. When I am away from work too long, I worry about the Angels. They find endless ways to need a doctor's care. I hope that Dr. Obermayer has been available to them during the month I have been out of the office, but I fear that he wouldn't go to them, and they wouldn't go to him.

We heard that Miss Harding is moving east with her parents. That means their little home will soon be available to the Eronen family. I love living at the Axton house, but it is definitely too small for Sev, Violet, and me plus the great furry mountain that is Koira. The Harding place is only two houses away, so my friendship with the Axtons will be easy to maintain. In fact, I will still have dinners here while Sev is at sea, as I love the family's company and am no great cook on my own. Birdie wouldn't allow me to move too far anyway, as she now believes herself to be Violet's big sister.

I have mapped what I think is our best route to the Lewis and Clark Exposition. I had time to do such things in the last month of pregnancy; it is as well that I completed the task before Violet took over my life. The King Street Station in Seattle won't be finished by the time we go, so I think Sev and I will ferry to Seattle, meet you two, and continue together down to Tacoma. It is a testament to how much I want to do this that I will get on a ferry again!

In Tacoma, we will board the Northern Pacific Railroad to Portland. They have a dining car that is said to be magnificent so we shall give it a try. And, this should be fun to experience: the

*train is loaded on a specially-constructed ferry to cross the
Columbia River. What a thing! A train on a boat. Two chances at
once to be motion sick. Do not worry as I will come with my
medical bag, prepared for whatever might ail us.*

*By the way, I have not forgotten that I have a baby in all the
excitement of planning our trip. Betty and Axe will take care of
Violet who will be nearly nine months by then and no longer
breast feeding. She will no doubt be glad of a week away from me!
That is the plan, unless I cannot bear to part with her and pack
her along in my medical bag.*

    Love to Timothy from me,

    Emma

After the maelstrom that was the early part of 1904, the
year settled down. Cutter appeared in her days and nights
less often now. Emma had time to consider events, not just
react to them. Grief, she realized, took its own good time,
and hers resurfaced on these days when she could give it
her full attention. She mourned her mother and her gran in
the evenings as she rocked her daughter. She looked for
their faces in baby Violet, but they were not there. Violet
appeared destined to be an Eronen...blue eyes at birth,
blonde fuzz, beautiful pink skin. Emma promised her
mother that Violet would be told about them, be strong in
her time as they had been in theirs.

She thought about her father, too, and how that quiet
man would have loved this gladsome, roly-poly baby. He
had been a botanical illustrator who taught her about the
flora around her. For that early interest, she owed him her
career. Emma still had a handful of his beautiful drawings
that had not been sold to *Curtis's Botanical Magazine* or
Wildflowers of America. These she'd kept flat in the bottom of
her trunk. Now she hung them on the walls of her office, the
bleeding heart and larkspur, the fireweed and feverfew. His

drawing of the western dog violet was hung in the Axton house, on the wall above her daughter's crib, a crib that had once been Birdie's.

Severin came home when he could, usually every third week. He wanted to take Emma and Violet to Canada at Christmas to meet his family. Emma absolutely refused to transport Violet on the sea...nightmares of little Virginia and Jack drowning in the swells haunted her. It led to their first argument.

"You are unreasonable on this subject," Severin observed.

"I am unreasonable on this subject," Emma agreed.

Instead, Severin's parents, brother and new sister-in-law came to them via ferry from Sidney on Vancouver Island to Everett on the Washington coast to Port Angeles. By the time they arrived, Sev, Violet, and Emma had moved to the Harding house so there was extra space, but the quarters were still none too large. It was not a particularly friendly visit, in fact, rather too polite. Emma found her in-laws to be a dour lot interested in little other than lumber and Lutherans. She did detect a bit of sparkle in the Finn newcomer, Helleena, and hoped the girl could manage to keep her spirit alive while helping Jorin push back on his domineering father.

The winter months passed. Violet grew, Koira adored her, and at Emma's office, colds, fevers, births, and wounds were business as usual. Finally, it was spring. The Lewis and Clark Centennial Exposition was just around the corner.

As was Cutter.

PART THREE

Lewis and Clark Centennial Exposition

Courtesy Oregon Historical Society

CHAPTER SIXTEEN

Oregon Penitentiary, Salem
Summer 1904

Portland began planning the Lewis and Clark Centennial Exposition five years before the main gates opened in June 1905. The colossal event would thumb its nose at Seattle and establish Portland as the premier business capital of the New West. Hundreds of acres were set aside for its grounds; no world's fair would promise more grandeur.

Fifty miles downstate in the Oregon Penitentiary, even Goodwyn Lewis was aware of the big doings to the north. Occasionally, outdated newspapers found their way into the pitiful prison library. He overheard guards talk about the money to be made on work crews, constructing the exhibit palaces. Grifters began appearing in cells, down-and-outs caught full of tales about riches to be made. Cutter listened to it all, storing it in the diseased recesses of his brain.

In the last days of August, he made his escape. Harry Tracy had bragged about how he did it, so Cutter followed that example. It wasn't hard. Besides, Cutter wasn't a closely watched prisoner, having been ill for months and causing no trouble otherwise. He was aware the guards considered him batty. How much effort would they make to get a crazy man back if he was careful not to kill anyone?

The evening of his escape, he conked an unobservant guard with a tool from the prison forge, raced to the oldest part of the yard, and climbed the crumbly wall. On the outside, he ran until he was exhausted. In the night, he broke into a general merchandise store, stealing clothes, food, a small amount of cash, and two hunting knives. The next day, Cutter avoided people when he could, but he purchased a ticket for the train to Portland. His goal was to fade in with the thousands of workers congregating in Portland. He would become one of them.

Even though crazed, he was cunning. He knew he must lie low until the prison downstate forgot him. He would not cause a widespread manhunt since he hadn't killed guards or settlers; law enforcement had too many other worries with thieves and confidence men congregating in the state.

Swampland was drained for the massive grounds of the fair, and a lake created. Dozens of temporary buildings were under construction along with new trolley lines, roads, and a bridge. Cutter hired on as a menial odd-job man, at a level where a strong back meant more than good references. There was no end to the work that could be done by a man willing to sweat for a living, something Cutter actually hadn't done since his days as a kid in Utah. But he did it now. He could drive spikes, clean sites, mend fences, lay shingles, use a hammer, make basic mechanical repairs. He kept his nose clean and his mouth shut. When he felt he was securely below the notice of the law, he figured he'd one day find his way to Seattle.

It was important to go there. He lay in a crew tent on a cot, muscles aching, through long wet nights, obsessed with the she-devil who fouled his life. She'd humiliated him, wounded him, stolen his gold. Emma was the source of his misery, and he would find no peace until she was punished.

* * *

The cold months of 1905 were easier for Emma's eclectic practice than the year before had been. In the sunny months, she'd harvested and dried plants, prepared tinctures, teas, and salves, so her supplies were more robust than her first winter. As her business grew, she continued to teach basic hygiene, in bodily care and in food preparation. It was an unexpectedly large part of her job.

All her patients mattered, but none so much as Violet and Birdie. Emma's botanicals helped with pain, infection, depression, but not with the childhood killers of diphtheria, tetanus, smallpox, measles, mumps, rubella, poliomyelitis. The list seemed endless. One mother of eight who sought her help had lost four children to disease. Another, three. Such killers were so far ahead of medical science that Emma could only try cleanliness to prevent, teas to soothe, and hope for cures. News of the baby punctuated all her letters to Lillian and Sev.

...Violet terrifies me with all the evils that surround her. I never before understood how motherhood meant living a life of fear...

... has learned to sit and to laugh, but is yet to crawl although I can see her considering such a maneuver...

... expresses strong opinions about anything but breast milk. I tried a bit of mush, and she acted as though poisoned, spitting the venomous concoction across the bodice of my newest dress...

... would prefer to be washed less often, but she will come to no harm unless I literally rub her skin off! I have recently read the word 'germ' and don't want such things living on my baby's surface...

... is mastering a flatulent sound made with her lips and tongue. This gives her much joy...

... has discovered Koira. He could already count to two, and was happy knowing his job was to look after Birdie and me. Now

there is a third mass of humanity added to his universe. His eyes express some confusion. However, he appears resigned to her pulling on his long hair when she cuddles next to him on the rug. I notice he keeps his tail tucked under and out of her reach...

While Violet was always on her mind, Emma did try for other topics lest nobody look forward to her letters.

...Willa has given me a beautiful basket, large and strong enough to hold the baby now or other necessities when she outgrows it. Willa said it is made of young cedar limbs and bark, then waterproofed with a glue the tribe makes from salmon eggs. The yellow, blue, and red dyes come from Oregon grape, huckleberries, and rotten logs. I must learn this process for myself.

Would you like a basket, Lillian? I have already requested the tribe make me another with a top to hold supplies too ample for my medical bag.

Willa has also offered to show me the hot springs far up the Elwha valley in the spring, and to introduce me to the variety of camps her people maintain. They seem to move up and down the river, following food supplies through their seasons, be it fish or game or berries.

I asked her the meaning of Klallam, and she said it is a word for something like Strong People. If you could see the devastation that alcohol causes them, you would be astounded. It appears worse for them than for us (even any Irishmen who might be reading my letter), so the Temperance Women would truly have their work cut out for them here.

I've heard people call the natives squatters which is detestable considering who was here first. In addition to being a taxi service for yours truly, they hunt, fish, farm, and trade their goods in Victoria and all along the coast. Crossing the great water in a canoe, from our Ediz Hook to Vancouver Island? Clearly, this is a braver group than I. Strong people, indeed.

April 10
Dearest Emma,

A strange occurrence happened here. For three days, our mail was taken from our post box, you know the one mounted on the outside wall next to the front door. Alfred found envelopes strewn about the porch. On the third day, he opened the door just as a man was rifling through it. Alfred says he looked rugged as a dock worker. The thief threw down the mail and ran.

I hope a letter from you or a bill or correspondence for a boarder has not gone astray. If I don't answer a question in one of your letters, assume it was lost and please make your inquiry again. I can only think a poor soul was looking for money. There are all sorts of petty crimes from pickpockets to robberies in the newspaper these days. As Seattle grows, so does the amount of ruffians looking for easy handouts, I suppose. Is the same true out in daisyville where you live or is the country safer from theft? I realize you are in more danger of bears! Mother says things just aren't like the good old days, whatever that means. Anyway, Timothy would like to install a mail slot in the front door if he has your permission.

Our Exposition is nearly upon us!
Lillian

April 20
Dear Lillian,

A mail robbery! Have you been receiving the type of mail that men want to steal? Dime novels of banditos, perhaps, or even worse? Sev tells me there are astounding postcards available, meant for men to view but never mail. Possibly Timothy is educating Alfred a bit too much!

I have been reading about our train from Tacoma to Portland. It is the Northern Pacific Railway and will continue its journey all the way to Chicago! That may be an adventure for another year. A brochure says, "the train's North Coast Limited service was

*inaugurated on April 29, 1900" so it is nearly brand new. This is
their luxury service, so we will have a very fine meal on the way
to Portland in the hoity-toity dining car. Imagine fresh linens
with china, silver, and five-star service, as we roll along taking in
the countryside! Sev says he might not know how to behave...I
assure him he is not alone! Who among us has dined on terrapin
soup, smoked buffalo tongue, or casaba melon? Fortunately, my
friend, there are many choices we have actually heard of.*

*Molly refuses to make more dresses for me, but she did create
a tweed travel suit since it comes closer to her chosen career as a
tailor, and because the French call it 'tailleurs.' The skirt is short,
no more than ankle-length (what a hussy I am) with a matching
jacket. I have ordered through our dry goods store a very large
feathered hat to accompany it.*

*In under three months, we meet in Tacoma. Do you suppose
Timothy and Sev will like each other as much as we do?*

So much to think about!

Emma

Sev was glad of baby news in her letters but also
desired her most honeyed words, not that she was as good
with them as he was. His letters were so unabashed, that she
rarely could share them with anyone else, but saved them
to reread for herself after Violet settled for the evening.
Female body parts had always struck her as basically
utilitarian. Through Sev's letters she learned hers were
objects of art. She was desired as she never had been before.
It made her giddy.

Do the other women I know feel like this?

Emma had read, in one of her more daring textbooks,
of a condition called nymphomania. *Dear God! Have I
contracted such a malady?* She determined to go through all
her botanical literature looking for cures. But maybe not yet.

She quite liked thinking about sex nearly as much as taking part in it.

* * *

There was no shortage of jobs. At first Cutter's crew worked on the pilings of the Trail. This street would be the location for the Midway. It climbed upward to the bridge that crossed the marsh which was becoming Guild Lake. Fresh water was constantly pumped in from the Willamette River. When the pilings were complete, the crew moved on to landscaping the dairy farm that would become the grounds of the great Exposition.

When the World's Fair in St. Louis closed, many workers headed west to help build the Portland fair. Cutter was never able to rise in status as new men flooded the foremen jobs; his frustration at this further fueled his anger at the world, but it also kept him below the notice of the law.

After working steadily on the Exposition grounds for months in the wet and fog, Cutter finally felt warmth of the sun just weeks before the fair was to open. The weather of a bright April chased the persistent damp and chill from his bones. He imagined steam rising from his back as though he were a racehorse after a workout.

Cutter figured it was time for his trip to Seattle. He told his straw boss he needed a few days off. It was important. His mother was sick. Because he was a good worker, this assistant to the supervisor said they'd take him back when he returned.

"If I fucking return," he mumbled, either aloud or in his own head.

His physical condition, if not his mental, had improved. The work was brutal, but in the fresh air, he managed to throw the chronic cough he'd contracted in the Penitentiary. It was sensual pleasure to draw deep breaths, unimpeded with the need to spit phlegm. In addition, his head wound, the one received from Minerva Prescott with a poker, and reopened with a swing from her daughter's bag, finally stopped seeping. It had bled and oozed, one infection after another while he was in prison. Now it was an ugly scar but clean and healed.

Cutter had a craving to see the Prescott Boarding House again. Maybe the bitch would be there, maybe not. But he was done with fearing her in his dreams and hallucinations. He would confront the hellion if he could. The idea of her had scarred his brain as much as the medical bag had scarred his head.

He took the train to Tacoma, then a far less luxurious branch to Seattle's Railroad Ave. This part of the rail was so overlooked and unattended, it was nicknamed the orphan train.

The Prescott Boarding House was an easy walk. For three days, in an alley across the street, he observed the comings and goings, mostly boarders he had never seen. Once he saw the fucking bog-trotter he'd tried to kill, and then he caught a glimpse of the pretty woman he'd seen there before, but no Emma. He stole mail each day, hoping to find an envelope to or from her, something that revealed her address. He found nothing. There were bills and letters for the boarders but the only letter in a woman's hand came from a Mrs. Severin Eronen.

In the entire three days, nothing hinted at Emma's presence, so Cutter finally wondered what he was doing here. He was at the end of the line. It was time to exorcize the Prescott women from what was left of his brain. It was time to give up.

But that left Goodwyn Lewis rudderless. He didn't have a Hole in the Wall gang as a base of operation, a partner named Tracy to lead him, the prison guards to tell him what to do, or a woman to draw him onward. Cutter returned to the only haven he knew, his job building the Lewis and Clark Exposition.

The straw boss was happy to have him back. "You're crazy enough to work on the Forestry building. Timber Temple, they call it. I call it damn dangerous, wrestling tons of fir logs in a chute from the lake to the site. You'll take it and be pleased about it."

Cutter took it. But pleasure was no longer a concept within his comprehension.

CHAPTER SEVENTEEN

Pier One, Seattle
June 27, 1905

Emma wasn't happy to board a ferry, but it was a necessary evil for their journey to Seattle. Everything about the vessel recalled the nightmare of the *Clallam*. Still, the day was calm, Severin was beside her, and the closer they steamed to the docks of the Emerald City, the more her mood lifted. She was eager to see her dearest friends and experience the adventures that awaited them.

Timothy and Lillian were on the pier when the ferry arrived in the Seattle sun. Emma waved frantically from aboard, attracting their attention along with nearly everyone else waiting in the line to load. When the four were on deck, striding toward each other, she bubbled over, spreading her arms in joy. "Look how dolled up we all are!" They were dressed in their finery, fit for high-class travel on the Northern Pacific Railway. Just a short ride on the ferry would shuttle them to Tacoma where they would board the train.

Timothy and Severin appeared too diffident and polite when they first met, at least until each hugged the other's wife. Their reticence soon passed, and all four began talking at once.

"So you're the Irishman who protected my wife from that vermin..."

"... you're the Northman who won her heart..."

"...lucky I found Sev since you were about to be taken..."

"...you cleared off so Timothy would be all mine!"

They were excited to the point of euphoria, their laughter approaching flighty. Emma imagined the other travelers on deck were delighted when the boisterous foursome adjourned to the vessel's little bar to celebrate, the men with pewter mugs of lager and ale, the women sipping Shipside Coolers of ginger ale, lemon juice, sugar, and fresh berries.

"Now then, how hard was leaving baby Violet?" Lillian asked when they were all seated at a table in the ferry's restaurant.

The young parents glanced at each other and Severin answered, "Actually, Violet appeared delighted with Koira and Birdie as we left."

"Yes, it's us who felt like howling as we bid her farewell," Emma said. "But I won't take the poppet on a ferry. Sev has graciously accepted that I find his chosen profession to be terrifying."

He shook his head with a snort, then for a while the men talked about the sea.

Timothy recalled his crossing of the Atlantic. "I took the first ship from Ireland to America that I could find when it was my time to go. I would have ended up in the New York gangs had my transport gone there instead of pitching and rolling around Cape Horn to get to the West Coast, so that is a good thing."

"The canal in Panama will soon shorten that route," Severin observed. "It must be a marvel to see."

"Far superior to the swells of the Chilean archipelago. Takes more of a seaman than I am to make a living that way." Timothy raised his mug in a toast to Severin.

Severin shrugged. "Puget Sound and the Strait are rarely so terrifying, well, except in the case of the *Clallam*."

All four paused, a moment of silence for lost souls. Lillian was first to speak. "I for one am glad to keep my feet on the ground. The train is the way to travel, most certainly." And so they dodged the dour mood that the unfortunate vessel could bring on. Even Emma maintained a chirky attitude.

For the rest of the journey to Tacoma, they studied maps and brochures of the Exposition, laying out a multi-day course that included everything each of them wished to see.

"We'll visit with the suffragettes while the men go to the electrical machinery exhibit..."

"...I understand there are scantily dressed dancing girls on the midway..."

"...far better than electrical machinery I reckon..."

"...does keeping your feet on the ground preclude riding a camel?"

"...if you're game, I'm game!"

A hired hack, drawn by a matched team of bays, took them from the Tacoma docks to the train station. It was a brief connection but they were glad of the transport so they wouldn't have to hand carry their suitcases, steamer bags, and hatboxes.

Emma, who kept her medical bag at her side at all times, was astounded by the amount of cases it took four people to attend an Exposition for less than a week. There were summer dresses of soft silks and cotton, at least two for each day, each with its proper hat. Chemises, drawers, corsets, and petticoats. Evening slippers with appliqué and lace-up walking shoes of medium height and pointed toes. In one of the cases she had even packed a parasol for walking the Exposition paths in case of sun.

The men needed two suits per day, although their travel clothes counted for one of them. Severin allowed himself the color of a striped waistcoat on this holiday. Emma had packed extra collars for his shirts since the detachable collars could be washed more frequently. She'd also tucked a boater hat for him in with her hats in addition to the bowler he was wearing now; she imagined Lillian had done something similar for Timothy.

The Northern Pacific Railroad was a major financial backer of the Exposition, so there was no shortage of posters and programs on the train. The train marketing team wisely displayed materials for all their stops across the country, promoting tourism, a new pastime to the middle class. The car offering their North Coast Limited service was a luxurious cabin indeed, with dark wood, brass fittings, and rich upholstered chairs bringing to mind pictures Emma had seen of fancy European men's clubs. The dining room, as advertised, was a five-star restaurant on wheels. "Take a gander at this," said Timothy, perusing the menu. "I've heard of some of these things after all. Roast beef, lobster, lamb and mint..."

During the chocolate eclairs, Severin stared out the large window and said, "Look! The train's boarding the ferry."

"So to sea once more, this time on wheels," Emma said with a touch of satire. "We can now both feel at ease."

"It's just the Columbia," Severin answered, putting his arm across the back of their dining banquette. "Everyone knows that rivers don't count."

"Keep an eye out for Lewis and Clark, paddling their way to visit their own Centennial," Lillian said.

"You have chocolate on your lip, Mrs. Crogan," Emma replied.

"Let me get that," Timothy said then kissed his wife in sight of any diner who cared to watch.

* * *

Still encumbered with luggage, they took a hack to their hotel instead of braving the new electric trolley that went to the entrance of the Exposition. As the horses clopped along Astor Drive, the foursome could see the massive event spread out to the right of them. The skyline alone was an astounding sight as though some magical culture had erected a fantasy to rival Xanadu, El Dorado, and Camelot. Enormous white exhibition palaces offered up Spanish Renaissance towers, cupolas, arches, and domes under the crown of red tile roofs. It was as gaudy as it was grand.

The 585-room American Inn was the only hotel constructed on the Exposition property, and Emma had booked it long ago. The finest rooms, the ones that cost her a staggering $6.00 each, were above the massive veranda and overlooked sparkling new Guild Lake. This was the luxury of gold; without it, she would have settled on one of the many new hotels off premise. "It really is a bargain," she justified to Severin. "The price includes the daily fifty cent entry fee."

It was not the first time that day that her husband laughed at her.

The trip had been long, filled with delights and adventures, so the two couples decided to spend the evening relaxing at the hotel. They sat on the veranda, watching night descend on the four hundred acres awaiting their exploration. The skyline was lit by 100,000 incandescent bulbs outlining Expo buildings like a sparkling lace border. Fireworks exploded behind the whole scene.

Emma was glad of her friends, her husband, and her baby safe with the Axtons and Koira. She drifted, considering the nature of joy. It had wondrous power, even more than the fiercer emotions. Moments like this were the reasons to struggle through fear and sorrow. This was the prize. This was the gold.

The morning dawned fussy. Emma thought her short cape and a large hat would prove more useful with her voile dress than her parasol. The American Inn was on the Exposition property so they did not have to come through the crowded main entrance, where 150 streetcars a day shuttled passengers to the gates. After breakfast on the veranda, they set out to walk the grounds once around as an orientation; if it rained hard, they would duck into the closest building and begin with the exhibits there. They strolled along the Lake Shore Esplanade, a boardwalk that edged man-made Guild Lake. Along the shore to their right were rows and rows of pink roses.

"Smells wonderful," Lillian said of the blossoms, inhaling a deep breath.

"Better than the swamp it was, I reckon," Timothy observed.

"The story of the New West according to the papers," Severin added. "Everything rosy, no longer crude."

Emma took his arm and summed it up by reciting the theme of the show as it was carved above the Government building they were soon to see. "Westward the course of empire takes its way."

Skies darkened as they walked. At the Bridge of Nations, they turned left and crossed to Government Island, where the federal exhibits and demonstrations were hosted. Thunder rolled, rain burst free. The four scurried into the Government Building, the fair's largest edifice, through the 200-foot tall colonnades, reminiscent of a Roman temple. At the entrance they came to a startled halt as they gazed up and out into the largest hall any of them had ever seen, a 70,000-foot cavern. Their plan to tour the full Exposition grounds dissolved away. Instead, there was enough here to keep them busy for hours.

"So this is what the government spends our money on," Timothy said, turning to view the entire panorama. "I've wondered about that."

Nearly every branch, department or bureau had an exhibit. It was a crazy-quilt of federal activities. The Mint demonstrated the making of coins, using all new electric motors. Emma was fascinated by micro-photographs and an actual culture of pathogenic germs in tubes exhibited by Public Health. The Department of the Interior fascinated them all with a stereopticon presentation on the national parks; the War Department displayed dozens of war machines, cartridge-making machines, armor-piercing projectiles, a model of Arlington National Cemetery. In a large tank with a glass front for observation, they demonstrated mines in a harbor so a battleship could not enter; timed explosions appeared to wreck the model vessel to viewer amazement. After that the post office seemed pretty tame with its display of every US postage stamp ever printed. But they spiced up their exhibit with the addition of items confiscated from the mail, including deadly weapons, bombs, poisonous reptiles and insects, toxic liquids, and opium.

Timothy offered to join Severin outside for the Life-Saving Services demonstration of boats, water guns, and buoys used in rescuing life and property from water. The very idea made Emma queasy.

"You go on ahead," she said. "I think I shall look for a cup of tea. Care to join me, Lillian?"

"Let's see...outside in the rain looking at hoses or inside, warm and dry, with a pastry? You gents go right on ahead." Concession stands were spaced throughout the building so Emma and Lillian soon found a spot to rest. The two friends needed time away from the men to catch up on the day-to-day of their lives.

"They seem to be getting along, don't you think?" Emma watched the stocky Irishman and lanky Finn head down the hallway toward the Life-Saving Building. "It's kind of Timothy to pretend an interest in the sea."

"I believe he is so glad to be away from my mother, and in the company of another man, that he is having a marvelous time. Now if Severin could just learn Irish drinking songs!"

Lillian assured Emma that her mother and little brother were happy as two mice in the cheese, knowing they ran the boarding house while the cat was away. "Alfred is finally growing through the know-it-all years and becoming pleasant to be around. Thought it might never happen! Of course, Timothy has had a lot to do with helping the lad along."

"And you, Lillian. Is he all you hoped for?"

Lillian munched a crust of pastry, apparently considering her answer. "At first, Tim seemed so...so there all the time. I am a tidy sort about my personal space, you know that. Making room for his clothes in the dresser and his shaving thingamabobs on the shelf and boots at the door has been somewhat harder than making room for him in my bed. Living with a man requires a great deal of room. But I now wonder what I was using all that room for. He is a habit, one I couldn't do without and have no wish to." She added sugar to the tea that a waiter refreshed. When he left, she continued. "There is one sadness, I guess. When you talk about Violet, I think I would like a baby even though I know

I am old for such a thing. But Timothy had his daughter and lost her in Ireland. Watched her die. He is haunted by it and will not go through that again. I understand, so we will be a couple happy with each other in a house full of other people's lives and dogs and an evil cat. How about you, Emma? Are you and Severin okay?"

"Oh, Lillian. Ours is such a different story. We had no real courtship, and I don't recommend that to anyone. But what little we did know about each other wasn't snippets like favorite foods or dances we favor. It was deeper, I suppose. We knew how we'd act in life or death situations, and how we could count on each other. After that, the little things seemed, well, little. He lets his mustache grow too long, he cuts his toenails in my presence, he rolls his eyes when he thinks I'm outrageous. It might annoy me, but I know he would die for Violet and me."

When the men returned they all went to the exhibit about the Philippines. It occupied a major part of the Government building because the islands only became an American territory eight years before, at the end of the Spanish-American War. The exhibit featured a village representing the islanders as little more than pagan barbarians. Emma found it more distasteful than informative. "I've seen our natives treated like this, and it is nothing like reality," she huffed to Severin.

"Do you suppose the women really wear blouses and skirts like that on the island?" Timothy scoffed. "Doesn't feel all authentic-like to me."

By late afternoon, they exhausted the Government exhibits, and the exhibits exhausted them. The weather had improved so they stopped for a meal at Piehl's, where they each had steak grilled on the Great Majestic charcoal range, an appliance provided to Exposition restaurants by the exhibitor.

The friends toasted the view and each other, then strolled back to the hotel to rest for the next day of tourism.

* * *

From the minute he'd seen the two men at the Life-Saving Services demonstration, nothing else mattered to Cutter. He'd been raking trash from the grounds when they passed by. He nearly gasped when he recognized that bastard Irishman he should have killed in Seattle all that time ago. The tall one looked vaguely familiar, too, but he couldn't say from where. Cutter followed them back to the Government building, watching their every move. Pretending to be there to attend to a plumbing issue, he trailed them to a concession stand.

And there she sat, like a queen among the peasants, laughing and enjoying her fine self. The wraith of his nights, the woman who outmaneuvered him at every turn. She pretended to overlook him, too unimportant for her notice, too lowly for her to fear.

Cutter was astounded to see Emma so out of place, at the Exposition, a state away from her home. Was he after her or was she after him? He was too crazed to tell the difference. Either way, purpose flooded back to his life. He would await his opportunity to cut her away from the men, like a heifer from the herd. Kill her slow.

Cutter followed them the rest of the day, back to their hotel that evening. He had a knife. Maybe he'd also get a gun.

* * *

After a day of informational exhibits, the friends were ready for a day of silly. The next morning, they headed for the Trail. This Midway was as tacky as any big fair, tucked apart from the area of classical architecture as if not to taint their cultural facades. The secret of that architecture, behind the faux marble and stone, had been revealed by *The Oregonian*. It reported that the structures were only plaster skin over wood frames. They would be torn down after October, when the Exposition closed.

Emma figured the Midway wasn't much more of a guilty pleasure than that. "You think this is the educational part of the Exposition?" Emma asked Severin, as he stared at a poster of strategically dressed dancing girls.

"I think this is the pickpocket part of the Exposition," he answered.

"Geez-o-Pete, the concessionaires will pick our pockets long before the crooks do," Timothy added with a chuckle.

They saw the hundreds of dancing girls and singing gondoliers at the enormous Carnival of Venice show, watched a horse that could count, marveled as two elks leapt into a tank many feet below. They gasped in fear as a high-wire bicyclist crossed Guild Lake. The women lifted their hems enough to sit on camels as they'd dared each other they would do. Severin and Timothy felt themselves hanging upside down by the Haunted Swing, a trick neither Lillian nor Emma chose to try. They ate ice cream waffle cones and popcorn, Severin won a bear for Violet at the shooting gallery, and they purchased souvenir coins, jewelry, and spoons.

It was in the Mirror Maze under flashing electrical lights, laughing at how fat or tall they could look and seeking the true pathway from the false, that Emma abruptly froze. The specter of Cutter appeared before her eyes, repeating and reflecting a million times in the glass, then gone. She swiveled back and forth, mirror to mirror, seeking him out. The others didn't notice her terror until she sucked in her breath and cried out. "It's him! Cutter! Did you see him?"

They didn't. Only Timothy would know him on sight, and he was as lost as the others. Nonetheless, as soon as they found the exit from the maze, he said to Severin, "I know him. If he's here, I'll find him. Stay with Emma and Lillian. Keep them safe."

Severin agreed. He and Lillian tried to calm Emma, to convince her that it was the heat and excitement of the day that must have overcome her. They found a bench and sat. In short order, Timothy returned, empty handed. "He's not on the Trail, Emma. Wherever he was, he is now gone."

Emma tried to regulate her breathing. She'd imagined seeing Cutter before. "It felt so real. He was there...like a thousand ghouls in those mirrors. I'm sorry to have frightened you."

Lillian gave her a soda to sip as her heart stopped its racing. Emma forced the image of Cutter back into her closet of nightmares. But the rest of the day was ruined for her, and she was furious with herself. *I'm not out of my mind. Why must I scare myself so?* She wondered if she was such a cynic that she couldn't let herself be happy for any too long.

Severin escorted her back to the hotel, while Timothy and Lillian continued to partake of the dubious entertainments along the Trail. As much as Emma asked him to go join them, Severin refused to leave her alone. They sat in the hotel lobby, watching the visitors, holding hands, pretending to smile, comforting each other.

"He wasn't there, Sev. I dreamed it. He's in my head, the opposite of an invisible friend."

"What can be scarier than a dream?"

They watched bellboys race about with messages, a housekeeper empty ashtrays, overtired children and beleaguered parents return from the fair, couples appear in elegant evening dress. Time passed.

Finally Severin said, "If I see him, I will kill him."

Emma said, "If I don't kill him first."

"Well then that is settled. But before we become partners in crime, let's go have dinner."

* * *

Emma slept remarkably well after her fright and awoke feeling refreshed and contrite. The day would be a busy one. They wanted to view more exhibits in the morning, and in the afternoon Lillian and she would hear Susan B. Anthony speak at the Oregon Building, promoting the agenda of the National American Woman Suffrage Association. For Lillian, this was the high point of the Exposition. Emma was happy to join her but, in truth she would rather attend the Pharmaceutical Congress that would convene at the American Inn soon after they left.

"Imagine! All those speeches on drug purity, toxicology, synthetics, manufacture of sera..."

"Yes indeed, imagine!" Timothy said. "I can imagine how you hate to miss humdingers like that."

"Better we learn more about women's rights?" Lillian asked innocently.

Severin said, "Give it up Timothy. You can't win."

"Oh, I don't know. While they give ear to the flapping of gums all afternoon, we'll enjoy demonstrations of EZ-use razors, keyless locks, fertilizers, and pipe wrenches."

"Good grief, what a dreary thought," Lillian scoffed.

They spent a lively morning strolling Lewis and Clark Boulevard, laughing and bickering about what to see next in the Forestry Building, the Oriental and Foreign Palaces. After a rest for their feet in the gorgeous sunken gardens, the gentlemen escorted the ladies to the Oregon State building for the Suffragette gathering.

"By God, look at them gather!" Timothy said, staring at all the stylish women climbing the steps through the colonnade into the building. "Like exotic birds flocking in so many feathered hats!"

"All right, all right." Lillian sighed. "You two go look at electro-doojiggers to your hearts' content."

Timothy feigned hurt feelings. "You don't want to see them with me?"

"No more than you want to hear the Suffragettes with me. Just drop us here and come back in a couple hours."

"Are you sure?" Severin asked Emma.

"I'm fine. Go with Timothy." Emma gave him a kiss on the cheek then a gentle push to his back. "In the morning, we'll only have time to see a few last things before our train for home."

It seemed a reasonable plan.

CHAPTER EIGHTEEN

Lewis and Clark Exposition, Portland
July 1, 1905

Cutter had followed Emma and her companion to the hotel the day before. Now he dogged all four of them from the time they left the American Inn in the morning. If the crew missed him at work, he didn't care. His time had come. The villainous Emma was right there with her friends.

Without warning, midday, the two men split away and strolled on down Lewis and Clark Boulevard. Cutter didn't know where they were going or why, but he rejoiced. The idiots had left the woman unprotected. He watched as Emma and the Pretty One blended into a crowd of their own kind at the Oregon building, then disappeared inside.

So many women on parade, he thought. *Who are all these bitches? Why aren't more men keeping an eye on them? What are they up to?*

He would act when Emma came out of the building. Cutter found a bench in Pacific Court, amidst abundant rose displays. He could observe from there.

Vibrant, sweet, his senses told him. Half a million pink hybrid tea rose bushes had been planted at and around the Exposition. Cutter knew. He'd planted many of them. *Vibrant, sweet.* Like these women in their fancy clothes, congregating together, paying no attention to him. *Not sweet. Dangerous women. Uppity women.*

He scanned the front of the building and sounded out the words on the banner that welcomed the National American Woman Suffrage Association. Here they preened, disrespecting all men. *Suffragettes. Suffer. Emma. Woman who causes suffering. Suffrage. Making me suffer. Shipwreck, prison, illness. Women make men suffer. Women. Witches.*

Cutter shook his head, trying to clear away thoughts that buzzed like bees, making it hard to think. He waited. In less than an hour, women streamed out of the building. Emma and the Pretty One, chatting with four others, emerged in one excited clump.

Laughing. Laughing at me?

The six women strolled right past him into the garden pavilion and through the entrance to the outdoor restaurant. Emma, his target, tucked in their midst, ignored him completely.

Roses. His roses. Suffragettes sitting together. Bitches.

Cutter should not be on the pavilion. A groundskeeper was out of place in his work clothes at this time of day. He stood out from the well-dressed patrons at the restaurant. He didn't care. He simply took visual aim at Emma, stalked past a hostess who couldn't stop him, circled the potted plants, the water fountain, the waiter stations. Cutter hunted down his target, stopping behind her slender back, where she was seated.

The others looked up, shock on their faces. As Emma began to turn, Cutter seethed, "Get up, bitch."

The women gasped at his words. They started to protest. "What's the meaning..." As a chorus they stopped together when they saw Cutter's gun. Like birds flushed from a hedge, they began to rise.

"Sit down, the rest of you," he snarled, loud and mean. "Quiet."

Emma alone stood, clutching her medical bag to her chest.

Cutter took her chair and sat. "Gotcha," he sneered at her then turned to look at them all. "Just like the boarding house. Six to sit. You to serve."

The six women sat still. The one closest to him whimpered, "I don't understand."

He set the gun on the table, pulled out a knife, and fast as a striking snake, sliced off the tip of her ear. She shrieked.

The rest of the tables on the pavilion went silent as guests and waiters turned to stare. The hum of conversation, tinkle of glassware, clink of silver all ceased.

"Now like the boarding house. No. Still wrong." He picked up the gun again and yelled at a waiter. "Get over here. Stand there, next to her." The waiter took a spot next to Emma.

"Now it's right. Six to sit, two to serve." He felt anger roll around his head like liquid poison. He couldn't think straight. "Still wrong. Still goddamn wrong." He swung the gun from Emma and shot the woman across from him. She slumped to the floor.

The others screamed.

He stood, aiming the gun wildly around the room. "Stand back," Cutter snarled at the restaurant staff and fair-goers who moved forward to help. They stopped, useless.

The busy pavilion was so silent it roared; such quietude was out of place at the boisterous Exposition. Distant laughter from the Midway mocked the terror in this place. Cutter shook his head at the crowd around him, then sat. "You're not here. None of you are here. This is the boarding house. Get back. Suffering. Suffragette. Stay back."

Finally Emma spoke. He turned to her as she spoke softly to him. "Hello, Mr. Lewis. Welcome to Prescott

Boarding House. Welcome back. Let's let these ladies leave while I serve just you. You'd like breakfast, correct?"

"Yes, yes. You serve, but they stay. Six at the table. Steak, griddle cakes, taters."

"Excellent, Mr. Lewis. However, these ladies have already eaten, Mr. Lewis. May they get on with their chores while I serve your meal?"

The terrified waiter beside Emma hadn't moved, but the Pretty One started to rise. "I will help, as well, Mr. Lewis. I run the boarding house now. Let our boarders leave so we can serve only you."

"No. You sit here next to me. She serves."

The Pretty One moved to the chair next to him, exchanging places with the woman whose ear bled profusely.

"Fine. We're all settled. I'll start you with a hot cup of coffee then bring your food, Mr. Lewis." Emma turned away to a service station and set her bag down on the counter. She opened it and put a hand inside.

"What are you doing with that?" Cutter yelled.

"Oh, just looking for sugar. I don't see it here on the counter."

"Why look what I found," the Pretty One said. Cutter turned from Emma to Lillian. "There's sugar right here. And look! There is the cream."

By the time he looked back to Emma she had moved away from her bag and picked up a tray with a cup and a pot of coffee.

Watch the witch. Tricky bitch.

"Get it over here."

"Yes, sir." Emma walked toward Cutter and placed the cup in front of him. "Now I'll just pour your coffee."

Sudden sizzling heat splashed on his head, his face. He yelped but that wasn't the worst of it. A piercing pain entered the back of his neck.

Cutter roared, but the pain didn't stop. It went deep, deep into his neck, into his spine. He heard his own voice crying, smelled the sweet odor of roses, felt the sun on his cheek as bright as the glisten of gold. Soon after that, everything stopped for Goodwyn Lewis.

* * *

Emma shivered as Lillian firmly wrapped her in her arms.

"It's Cutter's knife," Emma said. "It was in my bag. I used Cutter's knife to kill Cutter. Isn't that funny?" She knew hysteria was overtaking her.

Lillian held tighter as Emma began to laugh and cry. But this was no time to fall apart. A doctor was needed. Emma was needed.

The four other women were all suffragettes from the Braxton group. The two uninjured began to assist their two fallen sisters.

Emma pulled loose from Lillian. "Is Marian alive? Quick, hand me my bag." Emma knelt to begin emergency treatment on the woman who was shot, sprawled unconscious on the patio. Emma called more orders to Lillian. "Make Julie sit. Wrap napkins around her head. Press them tight against her ear. Find ice if you can. If she starts to faint, get her head between her knees." The waiter finally moved, rushing forward with a champagne bucket of ice and a stack of linen napkins to help Lillian with her assignment.

Two security men soon arrived. One sent the other for emergency services which were housed not far away. He knelt next to Emma and ordered her away. "Wait for a doctor, Ma'am."

"I am a doctor," Emma snapped. "Move away. Maybe keep observers back. Gather up the gun from the table."

The security man backed off, then followed out her orders.

News of the attack spread through the Exposition like wildfire. Among the first wave to come running were Severin and Timothy. They found their wives, summer frocks covered with blood. Timothy went to Lillian, moaning as he crushed her in an embrace.

"I'm not hurt," she said. "Please grab me more napkins from that table there."

Severin fell to his knees next to Emma on the patio. "Are you injured, my darling? How can I help?"

Emma wanted to stop, to allow her husband to hold her forever. But she needed him out of the way. "Marian is gravely injured. I must keep working. Can you make sure the man who is down stays that way?"

On the ground on his side was a dead man with a knife plunged so deep behind his head that it would be no easy chore to remove it.

Severin and Timothy both stood over him.

"Cutter?" asked Severin.

"Cutter," said Timothy.

August 4

Dearest Lillian,

It was a hard trip home. Without you and Timothy to negotiate the train and ferry for us, it would have been so much worse for Severin and me. Thank you, my dear friend. Now that I am back with my family and my business, my life is returning to normal. Who knew the Exposition would have such a shocking ending for us all. You will probably never travel with us again!

In the days since our return, Oregon has decided that, while I did kill Goodwyn Lewis, I am not to be charged as a murderess. Enough witnesses could give evidence on my behalf.

I wonder about it, of course. Did I have to kill him? Was I saving other people that day? Preventing danger to my family in the future? Or was I merely getting my revenge? Like the Oregon courts, I may never know for sure. But I can live with that...I will have to. Nightmares haunt me less often now. When Goodwyn Lewis died that day, he appears to have died in my dreams, as well. I don't envision the shipwreck victims nightly, and when I dream of my mother, she is most often happy.

Severin has earned a license as steam engineer so he is in more demand than ever. Violet scrambles on all fours with her patootie high in the air and threatens to take a first step. Koira grins at her as though she is his own pup.

I have made a decision about the Prescott Boarding House. I believe it is time for it to be the Crogan Boarding House. I would like to sell it to Timothy and you if you are interested. I am convinced that, at least for now, I belong in the beautiful wilderness of Port Angeles.

What a ride life has been, so crazily different than what I supposed it would be. Such a difference a bit of gold has made. It cost me the loss of my mother...but it led me to a medicinal practice that I love. It caused me to kill...but it gave me Severin and Violet. It expanded and deepened my relationships with an Irish rascal, an American native, fallen angels, frontier families, and my favorite suffragette! All in all, I think being a woman of the New West is a marvelous time to be alive.

For now I diagnose my needs as calm, routine, and quiet. Peace, I guess is the word for it. But the time will come when I will awake and think, dear friend, just what will we do next?

Affectionately,
Emma

-- THE END --

AUTHOR'S NOTES

Most characters in *Dr. Emma's Improbable Happenings* are figments of my imagination. Conversely, most events and locations are as close to historical accuracy as I can get, allowing a wee bit of wiggle room for creative license.

The outlaw Harry Tracy was an honest-to-goodness gun-slinging, train-robbing bad guy, one of the last of the Old West. His respectful conduct toward women - and his deadly behavior toward men - are both true to the legend, as told by newspapers of the day and promoted in books and movies ever since. The rest of the primary characters were developed by me to fit the known lifestyles and vocabulary of the times.

Eclectic Medicine was alive and well at the beginning of the nineteen hundreds. It was an expansion of the age-old beliefs in herbal cures, termed eclectic because it combined the use of botanicals with confidence in some surgical, prescriptive, and other medical practices. Traditional doctors pooh-poohed it, but that may, in part, be because its practitioners were often female; eclectic medical universities weren't all opposed to such a newfangled concept as women in medicine.

The Mercer Girls were a genuine part of frontier Seattle's history. They arrived some four decades before *Dr.*

Emma's Improbable Happenings takes place; Emma's fictional grandmother was a Mercer Girl. Single women came from the East Coast to Seattle at the invitation of Asa Mercer who was trying to balance the gender ratio. Several of the women were **suffragettes**, so the movement toward a vote for women was established early in the Emerald City.

The shipwreck of the SS Clallam - in the frigid waters of the Strait of Juan de Fuca - was an actual event. It was a desperately sad affair, shocking in itself and in fractious blame games that followed. Officials in the US and Canada could not agree whether the ship's captain was guilty of poor judgment or actual manslaughter. The list of passengers was never accurate; I felt comfortable adding Goodwyn Lewis and Emma Prescott to the people aboard that ill-fated day, January 8, 1904. Otherwise, details about the disaster are all from historical records and accurate as far as I am able to document.

The lighthouse on Smith Island functioned for a century, but its cliff eroded more each year. It was abandoned in the 1950s, and the last remains sunk into the sea in 1998. **The Newfoundland breed** was well established long before the setting of this book, so Koira might well have had working relatives wherever deep waters needed the bravest of canines.

The early 1900s were not the best years for **Port Townsend**, but it was a time of growth for **Port Angeles** (between floods and fires and following the experimental commune that existed there). As much as possible, I left the Port Angeles footprint alone, adding a dentistry office to the main street and an additional brothel a little way uphill.

References for **Klallam** lifestyles have all been crosschecked.

The Oregon Penitentiary was a hellhole, although probably little worse than others of the day. Harry Tracy was an inmate until he and a partner escaped, killing two guards and maiming others in the process. This actual event happened June 9, 1902, shortly before Tracy shows up at the fictional Prescott Boarding House in *Dr. Emma's Improbable Happenings*.

The 1905 Lewis and Clark Centennial Exhibition ran from June to October of that year. It was an enormous event, meant to turn the business and tourist eyes of the globe to the New West dynamo of Portland, Oregon. The exhibits I have described are from historical records, although a battle in the Garden Pavilion happened only in my imagination.

ACKNOWLEDGMENTS

There is no greater group of people than those who keep our historical societies up and running. They dig like badgers to extract the exact nugget that will make a book just one notch better. Often they are working from penciled journals faded to light gray, from arcane news articles, from photos so dark with age the images are nearly impossible. While I think all historical societies are goldmines, I especially thank the Clallam County Historical Society (Port Angeles, WA), the Puget Sound Maritime Historical Society, and Museum of History & Industry (Seattle). Kudos as well to the wonderful Facebook group called Historic Olympic Peninsula.

For sharing in the research and many trips up and down the Washington coastlines, I thank my sister, Donna Whichello. She is the silent partner in all my books, researching, editing, cheerleading.

My critique group of Heidi Hansen, Melee McGuire, and Jill Sikes puts up with me week after week. This is no small feat since I tend to the moody. They also babysit me through the angst of coming up with a title. I am seriously bad at that.

For this gorgeous cover, I am beholden to Veselin Milacic; for the equally attractive interior, my thanks to format developer Heidi Hansen.

I hasten to point out that any errors in text or in context within *Dr. Emma's Improbable Happenings* that may come to light are my own, the fault of nobody else.

ABOUT THE AUTHOR

Linda B. Myers won her first creative contest in the sixth grade. After a Chicago marketing career, she traded in snow boots for rain boots and moved to the Pacific Northwest with her Maltese, Dotty.

You are welcome to follow Linda on Facebook facebook.com/lindabmyers.author or email her at myerslindab@gmail.com.

CHECK OUT LINDA'S OTHER NOVELS

Fun House Chronicles
Bear in Mind
Bear Claus: A Novella
Hard to Bear
Bear at Sea
Three Bears: Short Mysteries from PI Bear Jacobs
The Slightly Altered History of Cascadia
Secrets of the Big Island
Creation of Madness
Fog Coast Runaway

Please leave a review of
Dr. Emma's Improbable Happenings
or Linda's other books on www.amazon.com.

Made in the USA
Monee, IL
19 June 2022

97563262R00136